PART-TIME LOVERS

FRIENDSHIP CHRONICLES 4

SHELLEY MUNRO

MUNRO PRESS

Part-Time Lovers

Copyright © 2023 by Shelley Munro

Print ISBN: 978-1-99-106333-5
Digital ISBN: 978-0-9941483-9-1

Editor: Evil Eye Editing

Cover: Kim Killion, The Killion Group, Inc.

Munro Press, New Zealand.

First Munro Press electronic publication August 2017

First Munro Press print publication July 2023

DEDICATION

For Paul, my partner in crime and fellow adventurer.

"Jobs fill your pockets, but adventures fill your soul."
—— Jaime Lyn

INTRODUCTION

NOW THAT NOLAN PENRITH is finished with the *Farmer Seeks a Wife* reality show, he's ready to get back to the farm and a normal life free of publicity. Normal also means resuming his relationship with divorced, solo mother Yvonne McDonald.

Except she seems determined to resist any talk of reconciliation. On to plan B: woo her to his way of thinking. And if persuasion includes plenty of raunchy sex, he's ready to man up.

Yvonne might still have feelings for Nolan, but she resents the way he expects to pick up right where they left off. Still, she's a healthy woman with a body that—damn it—melts for him, so maybe she can twist this situation to suit her needs.

All she needs to do is hold her heart out of reach, hold her head high, and enjoy his brand of lusty sex without a care in the world. Easy-peasy. At least until her plan gets a little kink in it...

Warning: Contains hot country loving between an arrogant, sexy farmer and a woman on a mission who intends to prick his confidence and slap him down—her way!

CHAPTER ONE

Lord, her feet hurt.

Yvonne McDonald thumped the spent coffee grounds into her bin and started making a soy latte and two flat whites. While the coffee dribbled into cups, she filled a teapot with peppermint tea leaves and poured over boiling water. She tried not to think about her cozy sheepskin slippers waiting for her at home.

The Clare town festival to celebrate the New Zealand spring was great in theory. Aunt Gina was cackling gleefully about their bumper takings this week, but they needed someone stationed at the door to draft customers into their bookstore café in manageable groups rather than massive herds. A set of the mobile yards the local farmers used for their cattle would do the job.

The bell over the door dinged a cheerful welcome. Yvonne didn't bother to glance up since they'd hired two students to help. The two teenage girls could do the smiling thing. She bashed her bell to signal order up.

"My feet hurt." Kelsey loaded her tray with the coffee, tea and a plate of fresh scones, jam and clotted cream.

"We need to hit Gina up for spa visits," Yvonne said, almost moaning at the decadent thought. What she wouldn't give for a man to greet her at home. Never mind the hot sex. She'd settle for a foot rub.

A flood of whispers stormed the café. Stray words struck Yvonne like bullets. *Farmer. Reality show. Susan. Nolan.*

"Yvonne." The familiar masculine voice hurled her into the past...

A dark bedroom.

Naked bodies sliding together.

Mind-zapping touches.

Pleasure storming her body, culminating in sweet, sweet bliss.

Stellar sex. Superior and awesome and stellar sex.

Another word bullet hit, and her head jerked up at the repeat of her name.

Nolan.

Damn, the man.

Her gaze settled, and irritation punched her in the chest, stealing her ability to breathe for a few seconds. She glared at Nolan Penrith, the bane of her life. Tall and lean from hard physical farm work, he was a male in his prime. His light brown hair—currently full of blond streaks from a fortnight of spring sunshine—needed a cut but he suited the unruly curls. His brown eyes sparkled with open admiration as he stared at her, and his sensual lips curved upward in a smile of greeting.

This acknowledgment with the underpinning of lust was a new development, and the hair lifted at the back of her neck in a silent warning to take care.

She directed her scowl away from his tempting smile and started to build the next order. A skim milk latte and a hot chocolate. Her disobedient mind refused to focus and like a rambunctious child, darted back to thoughts of sexy Nolan.

The man owned a farm on the outskirts of Clare and recently he'd brought fame and notoriety to the country town when he took part in the reality show *Farmer Seeks a Wife*. The minute he'd started dating women from the show, their...fling—the best description for their relationship—ended.

Kaput. A full stop on her sex life.

Yvonne frothed a jug of milk, the hiss and whir of the coffee machine overly loud and rubbing her nerves raw. The café section of the bookshop had become library quiet, but she didn't intend to glance up to see why.

She. Would. Not.

She sucked in a deep breath, tried to ignore the zing of sensual awareness tugging her breasts, the tremor of her hand guiding the coffee machine, the clamp of invisible

hands constricting her ribs. She brushed off her hormones'
celebratory rumba.

"Yvonne."

Cursing under her breath, she gave up the fight. She tore
her gaze from the steaming milk and glowered at the man.
"Nolan, what can I get you today?"

"I'm here to ask you to dinner," he said in a husky,
jump-in-bed-with-me-now voice. "Tonight."

Yvonne's mouth dropped open. Shock kicked her
square in the solar plexus while irritation charged like a
mad bull seconds later. "You have *got* to be kidding me."

Her voice emerged in a high-pitch shriek, the register of
her tone reminding of her of a squeaky cartoon character.
The customers in the café were pin-drop quiet now,
entertained by the impromptu *Nolan and The Dumped
Girlfriend* show.

Nolan straightened, his good humor visibly cooling. He
shot a glance to his left, one to his right. "No. I'm asking
you on a date. If tonight doesn't work, we can try another
night."

"You've treated me like a dirty secret," she snapped.
"And I don't need your mother's shrewish attention
focused on me again."

The man had rocks in his head if he thought she'd come
running after his behavior. And the way his witch mother
had flown around town on her broomstick to spread
rumors about Yvonne's morals. *Bah.* Elizabeth Penrith

might consider herself Clare royalty, but that didn't give her the right to treat people like crap for not measuring up to her lofty standards.

"Our dating has nothing to do with my mother. Look, we can't discuss this here. The café is too busy. I'll see you later at your place."

The bell tinkled as someone left the café.

Yvonne didn't blink. "I'm not a disposable commodity for you to discard then pick up when you have no better offers. I'm tired, my feet hurt and all I want to do is go to bed." Her good-for-nothing husband had left her and walked away with another man. Nolan had searched for a wife elsewhere. The third time was *not* a charm.

"You tell him, love," an elderly woman called from her table over by the magazine stand.

"Make him grovel," another woman shouted out her advice.

"Don't throw him away," a teenage girl called. "Give him a chance, or better yet, toss him my way."

"Make him work for you. He should apologize." Elderly Mrs. Wright added her two cents in a deep voice.

Yvonne felt heat rise up her neck to take residence in her cheeks and gave silent thanks to her Māori grandmother. Not many people would notice her discomfort.

"Tonight," Nolan repeated in a firm voice. He turned to face the café patrons and bowed from the waist, straightened and strode from the café. The doorbell tinkled for long moments then silence fell—a long one in which everyone studied Yvonne.

Ignoring the weight of stares, she focused on her coffee art. Once she'd completed her design on the top of her latte, she set the coffee on the counter. "Order up!"

NOLAN STRODE DOWN THE main street of Clare, past the florist, a menswear shop, an ice cream parlor and a store specializing in jeans. Everyone he passed stopped to stare, and he bit back a snarl of frustration. Now that filming on the reality show was over he'd hoped his life would settle into normal routine.

No such luck.

"Nolan. Nolan! Wait for me."

Nolan halted outside a real estate agent's office and waited for his mother.

"Lorna Wright told me you asked *that woman* for a date. In front of everyone." She started her lecture before they'd traded greetings. "How could you embarrass me like that? You need a wife of good moral character. I know several single women who are suitable."

"Stop," Nolan snapped. "Listen, because this is the last time I'm going to say this." He nailed his mother with a hard expression. "You will stop interfering in my private life. You will stop spreading gossip about Yvonne."

"I—"

"You will stop judging her, belittling her in front of other people."

"But she made you look stupid in front of the café customers. People are still speculating about the kinkiness you alluded to on TV. You must keep your head down."

After his recent behavior, Yvonne was due a few digs. "Nothing to do with you," he said, his tone uncompromising. "Leave Yvonne alone. Have I made myself clear?"

"But she has children," his mother said, furrowing her brow.

"So?"

"Someone else is the father. You don't want to bring up another man's children."

Fury jerked his shoulders straight. "I'm not you, Mother." His mother might treat Tyler, Nolan's younger brother, like crap because their father chose to have an affair. Nolan didn't intend to cast the father's sins on Yvonne's sons. He wasn't his mother.

His mother sniffed. "They're little hellions."

They were healthy boys who enjoyed rough and tumble play. "Stay away from them, and stay away from Yvonne. If I hear one more rumor, one more word from you about Yvonne or her children, I'll spread gossip of my own."

His mother gasped and her pompous air switched into disbelief. Some of the indignant color fled her face. "You wouldn't."

"Try me." Rumors and gossip were already circulating after his father moved out of the family home. "A few more juicy tidbits will add a pinch of spice."

Mother and son gazed at each other for an extended moment. His mother broke their visual connection.

"Very well," she snapped. "You make your own bed and lie in it. Just don't come running to me when the bed leg breaks." She swiveled and marched two doors down to the second café in Clare—the one she and her pals frequented.

Nolan noted the interest from passersby and huffed out a sigh. It was his mother's fault he'd gained notoriety in the first place. She'd sent off his application to the damn reality show.

He dodged a group of women who were pawing through a rack of clothes outside a ladies wear shop. A sale, the sign said. He hastened his pace. The glow in their eyes, their fervor served as a warning to any male with common sense.

Clear of danger, his mind headed back to his immediate problem. Yvonne.

He hadn't expected her to act with such hostility. He'd thought she'd understood he wasn't interested in the women on the reality show. Damn, the female sex was confusing.

Tonight he'd explain everything, tell her he wanted her, tell her he didn't need any other woman, tell her the two of them were in a relationship.

Together, they had a future.

YVONNE PICKED UP HER sons from the babysitter and drove down the busy streets to her small rented home, not far from Clare school. The recent reality show had put the town on the map, as had the news the show's producer intended to film again in the town.

A white compact cut in front of her and slowed rapidly.

She slammed on the brakes, her seatbelt stopping her from flying into the windshield. "Idiot!"

"Mummy called the man a mean name," David said from the rear seat.

Yvonne turned to check on David, her four-year-old, and Michael, her six-year-old. "Okay?"

"Can we have a puppy?" Michael asked, his earnest gray-blue eyes a mirror image of her own. His curly black hair, pale skin and slim build came from his father.

David took after her with light brown hair and an olive complexion. "Oh, yes." His brown eyes sparkled with enthusiasm. "We'd like a puppy."

"I don't think so. A puppy would get lonely while you're at school and kindergarten. They don't allow dogs," she said, forestalling their next logical argument. Her sons were the only good thing to come from her marriage.

The driver behind her honked his horn, and Yvonne muttered under her breath. While the surge of visitors helped local retailers, today the strangers and their aggressive driving were working her last nerve.

At home, she started dinner preparations and organized bath time, put on a load of washing and directed the boys to do a little tidying. She pushed thoughts of aching feet into the far recesses of her mind. Once the pasta was cooked, she poured over her meat sauce. It was full of disguised vegetables in the form of grated carrots and zucchini and diced tomatoes, so she was glad to see the boys eat with enthusiasm. One less battle to wage.

An hour later, with the boys in bed, she poured herself a glass of wine and collapsed on the sofa. She wriggled her toes. Sheer bliss. Then the doorbell rang. Yvonne groaned and pushed herself to her feet.

A few seconds later, she yanked the door open, her scowl deepening when she identified her caller. "What are you doing here?"

"I told you I was going to stop by."

Yvonne stood firm in the doorway. "I don't suppose you'd go away?"

"No."

Yvonne let out a heavy sigh and limped down the passage. She took a right into the lounge and lectured herself sternly. *Don't touch. Keep your hands to yourself. He'll hurt you again.* Her trepidation sailed close to panic.

Why had he come when she'd told him so clearly to stay the heck away?

She hesitated, glanced at the couch. No. No sitting. She didn't want him to get comfortable. She picked up her glass of wine and took a swig. The chair called to her throbbing feet. She ignored her aches and pains, the siren lure of comfort.

"Are you going to offer me a drink?"

"I don't have any beer. I used the beer you left in my fridge to make bread." Satisfaction tinged her words, the petty act still giving her pleasure.

His eyes glittered with amusement, and her hands curled to fists. The man stood on boggy ground. She was in the perfect mood to commit physical violence.

"Is there more wine?"

Ingrained manners had her stepping toward the door before her brain registered the act. Bother. She came to an abrupt halt, briefly thought about freeing the sharp words tickling her tongue, then continued to the kitchen. It wouldn't hurt to regroup.

The creak of the floorboards behind her straightened her shoulders and made her last steps to the kitchen self-conscious and jerky. *Drat the man.* Her hands were unsteady—again—as she retrieved a wine glass from the cupboard. The show of nerves continued when she poured the wine, drops of liquid sloshing on the counter before she regained control.

"Do I make you nervous?"

"You piss me off," she snapped. "I don't understand why you're here when I've made it clear we're over."

He propped his hip against the counter and studied her closely—until she felt like a creepy-crawly laid out on a microscope slide. She thrust the glass of wine at him and finally, finally, he released her from his gaze. "We're not over. I want you as much as I always have, and if you're honest, you want me too. Yvonne, we're good together."

Yeah, yeah. Her marriage had been agreeable at the start—pleasant and enjoyable even—but look how that had turned out. Not that she was bitter or anything.

"Yet you decided to publically search for a wife on a reality show," she said sweetly. "And when we were seeing each other, you'd come here, stay long enough to get your rocks off and sneak out again. I was a convenience."

"We're good together," he repeated, pinning her with his determined gaze.

"We fucked," she said with brutal intent. "We scratched an itch. I don't want that again. I refuse to sneak around. When I start dating again it will be with a man who doesn't act as if he's ashamed to take me out in public, a man who likes my children, a man who'll rub my feet at the end of a busy day. Damn."

Angry at herself for thinking of her ex-husband and for having to deal with Nolan, she limped back to the lounge and dropped into her favorite easy chair with a loud sigh. A man—this man—wasn't worth the aggravation of aching arches. Gingerly, she lifted her feet and placed them on the matching footstool. She closed her eyes.

Ah, the simple things in life.

"Why didn't you say you were exhausted?"

His harsh voice, right next to her ear, made every muscle stiffen. Her eyes snapped open. "I thought it would be obvious to anyone with half a brain. It's been a busy week."

"Look, I know I've screwed up, but I didn't apply to the reality show. My mother did, and by the time I realized, it was too late to pull out. My grandmother persuaded me it would be good for Clare, gain us some publicity, and I decided to play my mother and teach her a lesson, which is why I picked Susan. I like Susan. She's great, but she'll make me a much better sister-in-law."

"So it's true? Tyler and Susan are getting married?"

"Yeah." Nolan smiled—a wide and genuine smile that grabbed every one of her female hormones and embraced them tightly. Her fingernails bit into the flesh of her thigh to halt her impulse to touch.

"That's...ah...nice," she finished.

"My mother thinks she can direct my life," Nolan said. "I guess you've heard my father has moved in with me."

"Yes."

"Tyler and I learned a few other things recently. We're half-brothers."

"Is that why your mother is always so horrid to Tyler?"

Yvonne asked, curious despite herself.

"Yeah. Look, I don't want to talk about my parents. I want to make things right between us. I care about you, Yvonne."

Yvonne blinked to break their connection. She reached for her wine and ran her finger around the rim. "I have my sons to worry about. My aunt needs me. I...you hurt me, Nolan. I'm sorry, but I don't have the energy for a relationship. Not with you." The truth—she still hurt. Every time she'd heard gossip about that stupid reality show it had felt like dull knives ripping through her flesh. She wasn't dumb enough to put herself through the same pain again.

Nolan was silent for a long time. "I understand. Can—could we be friends?"

Her heart did a rapid dance, a victory bop against her ribs. Yvonne forced her brain to do the talking. "I don't think that's a good idea."

"Because we're more than friends?"

"No," she blurted. *Oh, Yvonne. Too quick.* She risked a glance at him and her heart did another crazy Snoopy dance.

A slow, very sexy smile spread across his lips, stealing her breath, filling her with longing. "What's that saying about the lady protesting too much?"

Yvonne squared her shoulders and prepared to lie.

"Would you like a foot rub?"

"What?" Aware she was gaping, she snapped her mouth shut.

Nolan lifted her legs and sat on the footstool. Bemused, she let him arrange her feet on his hard thighs. She swallowed, struggling with what to do, how to react. He plucked off her sheepskin slippers and dropped them on the floor.

"I don't think— Ah!" Her moan of pleasure reverberated through the lounge, accompanied by his soft laugh. Those talented fingers of his pushed and stroked, used pressure on the arch until every muscle in her body relaxed. He started on her other foot, and her head told her she'd be stupid to send him packing at this particular moment. Half an hour of foot rubbing and then she'd kick him to the curb.

"Is the bookstore still closed on Sundays?" he asked.

"No, but I don't work on Sundays." And she'd trained three local high school students who covered for her on Saturdays. She'd wanted to spend time with her boys, do normal things like watch Michael's rugby games and take the boys to the beach. Sometimes she managed to talk Gina into going with them, and they made a real family day of the outing.

"The local agricultural day is next week. Would you and the boys like to come with me? Dad is taking care of the stock entered in the show. I'll probably check in with him to see if he needs anything, but other than that, I have a free day. When Tyler and I were kids we used to look forward to the show. Tyler and Susan are going. We could have lunch with them. What do you say?"

"No, I don't think that's a good idea."

"The boys would love the rides."

Their friends were attending, and Michael had already started his pleas. Her heart overruled her head, and she wavered. "Are you willing to go on the dodgems and some of the other rides?" Yvonne loved the rides but found it difficult to supervise both her boys.

His eyes gleamed as he scented success. "Count on it."

Yvonne frowned, the grimace smoothing out when he started rubbing her foot again. A sound close to a purr rumbled from her throat. Her boys would love a day out with masculine attention. "Tyler and Susan will be there?"

"With Katey," he said, referring to his young niece. "Probably Josie and Eric as well."

Josie and Eric were Tyler's in-laws. They'd recently sold their farm and intended to move north to Auckland. Yvonne liked them both very much.

"All right," she said finally. "Where should we meet you?"

"I'll pick you up," he said. "The show starts at ten, but could you be ready at nine thirty? That'll give me time to swap the car seats over into my vehicle and check in with Dad at the show. Would Gina like to come with us?"

"She's going with a group of her friends," Yvonne

said while her mind struggled with the changes in him since their last private meeting. The Nolan back then wouldn't have known of the existence of car seats, let alone considered the time needed to swap them from vehicle to vehicle.

"Do you want to watch a movie?" he asked.

"Okay," Yvonne said, perplexed by this change in him. In the past, he'd slunk into her house and dragged her off to bed. An hour later, he'd left. No chit chat. No cuddles. No soft words. *Nothing but an empty bed and the sense of ill-use.*

"What do you want to watch?"

Inspiration struck. "I taped one of my favorite movies last week and haven't had time to watch it. *Romancing the Stone*," she said, watching him closely.

"Do you want a top-up of wine before I start the movie?" The man hadn't even flinched.

"Sure," Yvonne said. "I'll get—"

"No," he said, staying her with a gentle hand. "You wait there while I get the wine." He plucked her glass from her hand and strode from the room.

Yvonne studied the curve of his butt, which was faithfully outlined in a pair of well-worn jeans. When he disappeared from sight, she blinked, her heart thumping hard. She wasn't ogling. No, she wasn't. It was merely feminine appreciation of a nice, tight backside.

Thoughts of an earlier conversation with Gina popped

into her head. They'd discussed body language, and Gina had quoted from the book she was currently reading.

"'Women like men with broad shoulders and muscled arms, men with long, strong legs because we need them to provide food for us. We look for men with small, tight butts because that means they have good forward propulsion and are able to direct sperm and make lots of babies.'"

Yvonne shuddered. Nolan bore all the necessities, according to Gina's book, and especially the ability to pass on his sperm with excellent forward thrust. A shiver of heat dispersed through her body, frisking her pleasure points on the way to converge in an achy awareness between her thighs. She shifted her weight. It didn't ease her tension.

The movie, she thought, glancing around the room for the remote control. *Concentrate on something else.*

Nolan arrived back with their wine before she managed to struggle from the chair. "Stay," he said, handing her a glass. "I'll sort it out."

In his usual capable way, he had the television on and the movie queued to start. "One more thing," he said. "Hold on to your glass."

Before she could form a question, he scooped her off her chair and resettled her on the couch. He plopped beside her, and slung his right arm around her shoulders. She stiffened and knew he must have felt the strain of her muscles, but he merely picked up the remote and hit start. The opening credits began and soon Joan Wilder filled the screen. The actress was crying while writing the final words of her novel.

Every rapid breath Yvonne took filled her nostrils with his scent. Masculine with a hint of herb. Not aftershave, but the more subtle aroma of soap or a body wash.

"Relax," he whispered against her ear.

Easy for him to say. A romantic chick flick suddenly struck her as a poor choice of movie. Too much incentive to ponder hot and heavy thrusts. Yvonne sucked in a large breath and let it ease out in steady increments. The man wasn't trying to cop a feel or seduce her in any way. All he was doing was a little cuddling while he watched the movie.

Meantime, her thoughts took a corner onto a different street altogether. She thought about more forward thrusting of the naked, kinky kind, and the reaction spread through her body. The ache in her pussy grew, arousal dampening her panties. Thank goodness she knew this movie well and didn't need to pay attention. She drank more wine and stared at the screen.

Nolan might have rubbed her feet and talked her into an outing for the coming weekend. No way in hell did she intend to add the reality of forward thrusting to her crimes.

CHAPTER TWO

"I MISS SEX." YVONNE handed her friend Carol a caramel latte and propped her butt against the counter while she stared moodily out the front window of Carol's flower shop. For once, not even the sweet scent of erlicheer and the sight of bunches of tulips, standing like soldiers on parade in their containers, cheered her.

Carol's brown eyes twinkled from beneath a fringe that badly needed a trim. "I suppose we could give up on men and have sex together."

Yvonne flashed a broad grin at her friend. "Thanks for the offer, sweetie, but I like the working parts of a man. They might look weird face-to-face but I miss touching them."

"Well if it's just touching you want, I'm sure there are any number of Clare men who'd volunteer their man bits for you to grope."

"Ha!" Yvonne sipped her coffee and frowned out the window when she saw four women enter the bookstore. She crossed her fingers. If any more people entered the café, she'd need to end her break early. This time of the morning, after the breakfast trade, there was normally a lull. "I miss sex with Nolan."

"We put a hex on his male parts. We made gingerbread men and poked skewers in his likeness, remember? His tools don't work any longer."

Yvonne sighed. "I know. He came into the store yesterday and asked me for a date in front of everyone. I basically told him where to go, but he arrived at the house last night after I'd put the boys to bed." She heaved out another hard breath. "He rubbed my feet and watched a movie with me. *Romancing the Stone.*"

Carol's eyes widened. "Without complaining?"

Yvonne nodded. "And he asked me and the boys to go to the agricultural show on Sunday."

"Wow, sounds serious if he's taking you out in public instead of sneaking around."

"I don't think I can do this dance again. He broke things off with me to do the show and pretty much ignored me. His mother doesn't like me, and I don't understand what's going on with him now. He's changed the rules."

Carol set down her coffee, picked up a piece of greenery and deftly poked it into her spring arrangement. She stood back and circled the piece before giving a decisive nod.

"What do you want? You didn't like the sneaking around before."

"I want…" Yvonne paused and wrinkled her nose while she considered the possibilities. "I want a friends with benefits arrangement. I want lots of kinky, hot sex without complications, but I refuse to turn into a dirty little secret again."

"So preempt him. Before whatever he has in mind goes any further, spell out your rules. Tell him what you want instead of waiting for him to dick you around like he did last time."

The door opened and an elderly gentleman stepped inside. He frowned down at his hay covered boots and halted on the mat. His checked shirt and mud-splattered jeans, along with the boots signaled his farmer occupation.

"Don't mention dicks," Yvonne muttered in a low voice. "I'm frustrated enough already."

Carol barked out a single laugh before greeting her customer. "How can I help you, Mr. Rogers?"

"It's my anniversary next week." He produced a photo from his pocket and held it out. "Can you make my Martha a posy like the one in the photo?"

Carol took the photo and studied it. "Daisies. I can do that for you easily enough."

While Carol discussed the order with her customer, Yvonne sipped her coffee and thought about sex and Nolan.

Friends with benefits.

That would be perfect. If she knew the rules going in, her heart would remain stanch instead of getting trampled beneath Nolan's gumboots. *Yeah.* She'd tell him what she wanted when she wanted, and if he didn't play by her rules he could find another tame woman to prime his man parts.

"I WANT SEX," YVONNE said the second Nolan entered her house. She shut the door with a firm click and turned to him, crowding into his personal space.

Bemused at the change in her attitude—her willingness—he took half a step back, and his spine connected with the wall. She kept coming until her breasts pressed against his chest and her hands curled around his biceps. His dick twitched with interest, and when her lips covered his, all his blood shot south, crowding into his cock in a pained rush.

Her kiss was skilled, familiar, her lips firm over his. Her tongue traced his bottom lip and danced across the seam in a bold demand for entrance. He, of course, didn't have an ounce of argument in him—not with his cock directing proceedings. His hands skimmed down her back and settled on her lush arse. He pulled her tight to his hardness, his mind racing with fervent prayers of thanks.

God, it had been so long. This woman, she did it for him,

and the months since they'd last been together told him he couldn't—wouldn't—settle for a replacement.

She was it.

He loved the taste of her, the look of her and her quick mind kept him entertained. Oh yeah. She was perfect for him, and he didn't give a flying fuck what his mother thought. He was an adult, and this time he intended to go after his treasure.

Yvonne.

Yvonne's boys.

A family.

His family.

She pulled out of the kiss, her harsh breathing telling of her arousal. "Let's go to bed."

Still in shock at her easy acquiescence, he trailed her like a friendly puppy, letting her tug him down the dark passage to her bedroom. Luckily for both of them, her boys were heavy sleepers. As much as Nolan enjoyed the boys' company and their endless supply of questions, this night was for him and their mother.

In her bedroom, she flicked on one of the bedside lamps. A warm glow highlighted the double bed with its silver cover and the contrasting purple pillows. She tossed the fancy cushions on the floor and started shimmying out of her clothes.

Nolan stared, mesmerized by the unveiling of her body. The full breasts, the creamy milk-and-coffee skin that told of her Māori blood. So stunning. So pretty. A trim waist that didn't show much evidence of the two babies she'd carried, the flare of her hips. Womanly hips that were perfect for him to grip while in the throes of passion. Her jeans hit the floor to reveal long legs. Her feet were big and she often complained about finding shoes to fit. He smiled at the bright red toenails. *Sexy*.

"Are you going to spend all night staring?" Her voice was a husky purr of objection. "I can always get out my vibrator."

She was kinky fun in bed and game to try anything. They'd laughed a lot in this bed, and they'd had some risqué, seriously hot encounters.

Nolan started on his clothes, his eyes narrowed as he watched her feminine grace. She raised her arms in a lazy stretch, then freed her hair from its tight knot at the back of her neck. The brown locks fell halfway down her back.

Yvonne climbed onto the bed and parted her legs to reveal trimmed curls and pretty pink flesh. She'd shaved, and he stared at her folds and the glistening juices that already coated her skin. Her finger slid down to circle her clit. "Sex," she said. "You remember how to do it?"

Nolan unzipped his jeans and yanked them down his legs. A swift curse rang out when he realized he still wore his leather boots. He did an ungainly, one-legged dance while he rectified the situation.

"You want to taste me, Nolan?"

"Yes," he snapped, wondering when the hell he'd lost control of this encounter.

Naked—finally—he moved between her legs and boosted her higher with his hands beneath her arse. He settled in to feast, her sweet yet musky flavor bursting across his taste buds.

"Yes," she said. "Suck my clit." Her hands grabbed for his head, fastened on his ears and using them like handles, she tried to direct proceedings.

Grinning against her flesh, he used his tongue to circle the swollen bud, not giving her exactly what she wanted.

"Nolan." She yanked his ears. Hard.

"*Ow*, woman."

"Give me," she demanded.

He swept his tongue over the straining bundle of nerves. Once. Twice.

Her hips canted upward, into the pressure of his mouth. She groaned, long and loud, her hips jerking with the force of her release. Nolan backed off on the direct stimulation, giving her just enough to draw out the orgasm.

Her lashes flickered, and she opened her eyes. Without warning, she twisted her body away. Her eyes gleamed when she met his gaze. "On the bed. Flat on your back."

Nolan stared, part of him shocked. *Who is this woman?*

A sharp crack across the side of his buttock made him start, and this time he blinked.

"I believe I said I needed you flat on your back."

Slowly, Nolan crawled up the bed and turned over. Immediately, he sought her gaze while wondering what the hell was going on. She'd hit him. His arse still tingled from the contact.

She studied his body, and he watched her do it. She smiled and leaned over to trace his lips with her fingertips. He sucked one fingertip inside his mouth, his lips working the single digit in a very sexual way.

A quick gasp escaped her, and she let him continue for a few seconds longer before pulling away. She explored his chest with her hands, and he sucked in his breath, his balls so hard he thought they might burst. But he forced himself not to move and let her continue to take the lead.

Her tongue flicked over a nipple. Back and forth she licked, worrying the flat disc until he shuddered. She ignored the other and moved down his body. Yes. She was going to touch him, put an end to the months of sexual drought. Instead, she blew a stream of warm air along the length of his dick, the final burst hitting the crown. Another tremor swept him as cool fingertips tugged his sac.

She pulled back, removing her touch almost as soon as she'd started. He was about to object, but swallowed his complaints when she retrieved a box of condoms. She ripped one foil packet open and sheathed his cock in a quick, efficient manner.

He started to move, but she stilled him with a hand on

his hip. She straddled his body and guided his cock to her entrance, pushing down a fraction until her scalding hot pussy choked the head of his dick. It was the best of times and the worst of times...

What the fuck?

She'd scrambled his brain. Yeah, his recent abstinence had shorted something. Why else would he mentally quote some long dead writer in the middle of getting laid?

He gave himself an invisible head slap—an intellectual kick start.

Yvonne took a fraction more of his cock.

Oh, yeah. "God, Yvonne. Take me deeper, please." He eyed her breasts. "Lean over so I can suck your tits."

She gave a breathless laugh and sank down an increment more. He groaned and his hips rose. He surged deeper into her heat, and it felt so bloody good he thought he might explode.

"You feel good inside me," Yvonne said. "You fill me, make me ache. I want to go slow, but it's *sooooo* hard."

Nolan didn't know if she was talking about his cock or her trouble going slow. Didn't care. His hips rose in a hard thrust until he was embedded balls-deep in her moist heat.

Yvonne sat back on her haunches and wriggled around a little. Then, to his great relief, she started to ride him with a fast up and down. With her head thrown back and her breasts playing peek-a-boo in her hair, she was a real picture, a visual he'd certainly recall tomorrow during his work day.

Didn't seem as though he was gonna get to taste her breasts, though. *Later.*

Part of him wanted to close his eyes to savor the current of pleasure swamping his senses. But Yvonne swaying above him was a sight to behold. He forced his eyes to remain open and watched her pull her bottom lip between her teeth, her long hair flowing around her shoulders. The scent of sex and arousal floated around them and combined with the lingering citrus of a furniture polish.

She slid her hand down to where their bodies joined and combined some finger action with her frantic up and down. Her breath hitched, and the vision and sensations were too much for Nolan. He came hard, his seed spurting from him in almost painful contractions. Her vagina pulsed around his dick, the tight grip extending the length of his orgasm. A cry of pleasure emerged from deep in her throat, gradually settling a humming note.

God, she was beautiful. Maybe not in the traditional sense, but when she smiled, or times like now, with the bloom of release flushing her skin, she was a stunner.

She leaned toward him and he drew her against his chest, wrapping his arms around her sweaty body. She sighed, and contentment filled him. He'd stupidly allowed his mother to maneuver him into the reality show. He'd hurt Yvonne, made her doubt him. His arms tightened momentarily before he caressed her back. She'd obviously forgiven him, and now they could move forward into the future.

Yvonne stirred, pushing back to clamber off him. She flashed him a grin, and he found himself responding in kind.

Nolan took care of the condom and held out his arms. "Come here."

"What's the time?"

Nolan glanced at his watch. "Almost nine."

"Okay. My favorite TV show is on at nine-thirty. Thanks for the sex. It was great."

"What?" Nolan was pretty sure his face wore a stunned expression.

Yvonne picked up his shirt and handed it to him. "We both needed sex. We had it. End of story."

"But...but..." Good god. He was stuttering.

Yvonne thrust his boxer-briefs and jeans at him. "This new arrangement will work much better."

"What arrangement?" His voice was faint, his brain juddering because he was missing his normal smooth gear changes.

"Friends with benefits," she said. "Yes, I think this will work perfectly. Show yourself out. I don't want to miss the start of my show."

Nolan gaped after her. *What the fuck?*

CAROL LAUGHED UNTIL SHE cried, and Yvonne's mouth twitched as she reached into her handbag for a packet of travel tissues. She passed them over to her friend and waved away the waitress with a quick nod of her head.

"We'd better decide what we want to order," Yvonne said.

Still smirking, Carol picked up her menu and scanned the contents. "The scallops and salad," she said decisively. "So you thanked him politely for the sex and ordered him to leave."

Yvonne took a sip of white wine. "When he tried to talk to me before he left, I told him I'd ring when I felt the urge for more bedroom gymnastics."

Carol leaned forward, her eyes big and bright. "You didn't."

"I also told him I'd ordered some new sex toys and some wonder cream that's meant to do interesting things to a woman's libido. I told him to make sure he got plenty of rest." A gurgle of amusement rang out. "You should have seen the look on his face."

"No!"

"Then, I turned my attention back to the historical costume drama and ignored him until he left."

"Has he contacted you since?"

"No, but the agricultural day is tomorrow. I'm assuming he'll still take me and the boys."

"And if he doesn't turn up?"

"I'll take the boys myself and grab my best friend to help me control my two excited sons when they want to head in opposite directions."

"Deal," Carol said. "What's your next move?"

"I want to keep him off-balance. I really did order some sex toys, so if he doesn't take us to the show, I'll give him a call in a couple of days and invite him over to help me test out my purchases."

Carol cackled and dabbed at her eyes again. "I need to find a man, too, one that performs on demand."

"Anyone in mind?"

"Not really. The new vet seems nice, but he already has a welcome party of single females in the surgery. My cousin works as receptionist-nurse and she said the domestic pets in Clare have mysteriously developed rare diseases and require immediate treatment. They've never been so busy."

"Maybe someone interesting will arrive with the film crew doing the reality show about the Shakespeare sextuplets."

"One can but hope," Carol said in a prim tone.

NOLAN SPENT THE REST of the week mustering sheep and moving the flock down from the hill paddocks to prepare for early lambs. The weather forecast was good, which made him happy. While he arrived home dog-tired, he spent his nights twisting and turning, his mind replaying the last time he'd seen Yvonne.

He fed his three dogs, checked their water and walked to the house. He pushed open the rear door and pulled off his boots before he entered the kitchen.

She'd thanked him for the sex and dismissed him.

Now, the night before the start of their date, he wasn't sure what to do. Did he turn up at Yvonne's place as discussed?

Thanked him for sex. His snort echoed through the kitchen.

Samuel Penrith, his father, glanced up from where he sat and rose. "Didn't think you'd ever finish. Want a beer and a shower before you eat?"

"A couple of the yearling heifers got out on the road." Nolan shrugged. "They didn't want to go back into their paddock." Nolan opened the fridge and pulled out a beer. "I'll grab a quick shower. I can smell myself and it isn't pretty."

In the bathroom, he stripped off his dirty clothes and stuffed them into a hamper. He'd need to put on a load of laundry later tonight.

The water took long minutes to run hot, but Nolan didn't bother waiting. He took a quick sip of beer, set the can aside and stepped into the shower. Cold water cascaded over his shoulders and down his back, the temperature gradually heating and relieving some of the fatigue in his muscles.

Talk about a surprise. She'd mentioned next time and added a spiel about sex toys. He had to admit his mind hadn't heard much past the sex toys. A woman couldn't expect a man to process conversations when she lobbed verbal bombs. And kinky ones at that. He really liked that about Yvonne—sexually, she was a fireball.

Blood crowded his cock, and he ignored his erection. He grabbed the soap and started to wash with brisk, economical movements, thoughts of Yvonne swirling through his mind.

On Sunday, he'd go and pick up her and the boys, just as they'd arranged earlier. Yeah, he'd proceed as he'd planned and play the day by ear. He'd get her in private at some stage during the day and demand answers.

God, why would she thank him for sex anyway? They'd had sex before—quite a lot of it before he'd participated in the reality show. She'd never thanked him. He hadn't given polite appreciation either. They'd had mutual respect, exhausting each other while they'd burned up the sheets. A couple of times they'd both fallen asleep and the boys had almost caught them together.

She hadn't expressed her gratitude then. No, she'd woken him abruptly and kicked him out of her bed. *Women.*

God, they confused him.

Dressed and back in the kitchen, Nolan grabbed another beer. The scent of tomatoes and rich gravy filled the air, a hint of garlic and basil.

"I'll serve dinner," his father said, pulling a casserole dish out of the oven.

"Thanks for cooking," Nolan said.

"I enjoy it," his father said, surprising Nolan.

"You do?"

"Your mother would never let me in the kitchen. I thought about training to be a chef rather than following my father's footsteps. My father had very firm ideas about the roles of men and women."

"Yeah?" Nolan passed his father the warmed dinner plates. Since his father had moved out of the family home, they'd become closer. His father had bloomed—for want of a better word—since he'd split from Elizabeth. "Where did you get this recipe?"

"Looked it up on the net," his father said as he dished up the mashed potato, boiled peas and some sort of casserole. "I like trying new things."

Sure as hell beat coming in late and cooking for himself. "Are you going to try to make up with Mum?"

"It's too late. I hate the way she drove Tyler away. I share the blame because I didn't stand up to her. I'll have to deal with the guilt for the rest of my life."

"How are things with you and Tyler?"

"He's wary, and I don't blame him. Josie told me once

the farm is sold all of them are moving to Auckland."

"Tyler always preferred art to farming."

"He takes after his mother," his father said. "She had a passion for art."

Cooking was a form of art, no matter what his father said. "You could always go up to Auckland for a holiday. There's nothing to stop you visiting Tyler." Nolan's phone beeped to indicate an incoming message. He ignored it and continued working on his pile of mashed potato. "This is really good."

"It's a small way to pay back your support, son." Samuel ate some of his own meal. "I don't mind taking responsibility for the cooking and shopping. Beats tromping through the mud with my gammy leg."

Nolan's phone beeped again.

"Do you need to get that?"

"Later," Nolan said. "I'll help with the dishes."

His father beamed. "I made apple crumble."

It was almost two hours later when Nolan retired to his bedroom and set the alarm. His phone beeped and he plucked it from his pocket, hitting a button to illuminate the screen. Yvonne had sent him a text. Several texts.

R u ignoring my txts?

He scrolled down, his eyes widening when he read the other two texts and studied the attached photos. The first one showed a bright blue vibrator and something that looked like a butt plug. There were a couple of other items in the photo, which were difficult to identify. The message said, *My sex toys arrived. We need to make a d8 2 try out.*

Nolan scowled at his screen. So she could thank him again in that oh-so-polite tone. His hand fisted around his phone, and he had to force himself to unclench his fingers and check the next message.

Sat night, around 8? The attached photo showed deep cleavage, and immediately his cock went to half alert.

The woman was trying to kill him.

She'd changed, and he had no idea what to make of the sultry beauty who'd taken her place.

Nolan cleaned his teeth and shucked his clothes in preparation for bed. He turned his head to stare at his phone where he'd left it on the bedside cabinet. *Ring her.* Without a second thought, he picked up his cell and hit speed dial. Yvonne answered almost immediately.

"Hello."

"It's me," he said gruffly. Had her voice always sounded so husky?

"Ah, I thought you'd decided to ignore me."

"I was late getting in tonight. Dad and I were eating dinner."

"How is he?"

"Fine." He didn't want to discuss his father or his parents' failed marriage.

"I'm feeling naughty tonight. I'd ask you to come over, but we've both got an early morning tomorrow. You are still picking us up?"

"Yeah, nine thirty," he confirmed, smothering a yawn. It had been a long day.

"Would you sleep better if I talked dirty to you?"

"What?"

She laughed softly. "What are you wearing?"

"Nothing."

"Right," she said briskly. "I want you to turn off your light and climb into bed. Get yourself comfortable and put your phone on speaker. Imagine I'm there with you, my lips on yours, my hands roaming your body."

With her husky voice purring suggestive things in his ear, it didn't take long for blood to race to his dick.

"Curl your hand around your cock, stroke it. That's me," she whispered. "Holding your steely strength with just the right amount of pressure."

"Steely strength?" Amusement threaded his voice.

"Yes, that's the way you always feel to me. Warm and hot and strong."

Emotions curled through his chest. There was amusement and respect and caring, but along with those emotions came joy. Yvonne was...

"I take you in my mouth and rub over your crown with my tongue. You like this so much that pre-come is already beading at your slit."

Yvonne was a siren sent to seduce him. Unbidden, he started to stroke himself, falling under her spell. He felt the tension riding his shoulders sink down his body to converge in his groin. His hand slid up and down, the initial dry strokes soon smoothed by pre-come.

"My tongue is stroking your sensitive underside each time I take you into my mouth. You can feel the heat of my mouth, the tight seal of my lips. When you look down at me—did I mention I'm kneeling at your feet?—the visual is as much a turn on as my mouth around your cock. You meet my gaze and hold it. Your legs are planted firm, but your breathing is fast. Your pretty eyes are glittering with passion. Your fingers thread through my hair—"

"Is it loose?" The silky drift of her hair against his skin never failed to get to him.

"You spear your fingers through my curls, holding my head in place, directing the way I suck you."

Nolan's balls tightened to the point where he knew that no matter how tired he was, he would come...or lie awake for the rest of the night.

"I'm taking you deep now, almost to the back of my throat and it's absolutely perfect. I'm breathing through my nose and taking you easily. Feel the delicious slide against my tongue, the tight suction of my mouth."

Oh yeah. He could feel it. Nolan closed his eyes and sank further into the fantasy, letting the low tone of Yvonne's voice seduce. He worked his shaft with his callused hand, his fingers a tight vise.

"Your legs start to tremble and your breathing changes. I

know you're getting close. You're talking to me, telling me I'm doing a good job and my mouth feels good. Wet and tight and perfect."

Nolan hissed, wondering briefly why they hadn't done this before. The thought swirled away, replaced by the tight pressure of impending climax. His muscles were tense, his balls pulled high and tight, his breathing hoarse. Excited.

"I add a swirl of my tongue, a different move than what I've been using. You groan."

Nolan moaned on cue, so close to orgasm he wondered if his heart might gallop out of his chest. He continued the hard strokes, the pulls at his dick while he listened to Yvonne's sexy purr.

"I take you extra deep and swallow around the tip of your throat. You hold my head tight so I can't move. I don't struggle and long moments later, you pull out and slide inside again. I swallow and with a roar, you come down my throat."

Nolan's climax burst from him at her demand—hard and painfully good—semen shooting over his palm and fingers. His heart hammered his ribs, the contractions of his cock taking a long time to subside.

"I manage to swallow most of your come and start to lick you clean, but you tell me you're too sensitive and you need to sit before you fall because that was some supreme head."

Nolan chuckled and used the corner of the sheet to wipe up the mess. Another item to add to the laundry tomorrow.

"You pull me up and kiss me, wiping a bit of come off the corner of my mouth." She paused before continuing. "Sweet dreams, Nolan. We'll continue this tomorrow night in my bedroom. You can have dinner with us after the agricultural show, and we'll go from there. Sex toys optional." Pure naughtiness wrapped around her tone before a click indicated she'd hung up.

"Damn," he muttered. Score another to Yvonne, the sultry temptress. She was turning him inside out, pulling him off-balance. Nolan resettled in his lonely king-size bed. Part of him looked forward to tomorrow—the sudden challenge Yvonne had thrown into their game. The other part of him was bloody terrified.

CHAPTER THREE

YVONNE ORGANIZED HER SONS, and by nine thirty David and Michael were waiting for Nolan to arrive, both boys constantly peering out the window and bouncing around in their excitement.

The phone rang and she picked up, hoping it wasn't Nolan to say he needed to change plans. Her boys would mutiny.

"Gina," she said in relief when she heard her aunt's greeting.

"I've packed a picnic basket for you," her aunt said in a gruff voice. "Make sure you get Nolan to stop by to pick it up."

"I was just going to grab some muffins and a few sandwiches," Yvonne said.

"Don't argue, Missy," her aunt said in her forthright way.

Gina Muir might scare a lot of people with her blunt attitude, but Yvonne knew the woman hid a heart of gold beneath her no-nonsense exterior.

"Thank you. Are you sure you don't want me to come back and relieve you?"

"It'll be quiet. It was yesterday. I intend to close early, probably at two after lunch. That's plenty of time for me to check out the displays in the Food Hall and meet with my friends. Enjoy your time off. You work too hard."

Anyone else might have focused on the abrupt delivery. Yvonne heard the concern and caring and her heart swelled with love. Gina had been her savior after her marriage fell apart, offering a job and a new life, and Yvonne would never forget her aunt's generosity.

A car sounded outside in the driveway.

"He's here!" Michael shouted.

"Yahoo!" David hollered.

Both her sons ran for the door in a full-on race with thumping feet and yells of jubilation.

"Nolan has arrived," Gina said, hearing the racket. "Don't forget to stop by the store."

"See you soon, and thanks."

"No thanks necessary," Gina said and hung up.

Yvonne picked up her handbag, plus jackets for herself and the boys. She walked through the open door and smiled at the way the boys gamboled around Nolan like playful puppies. He'd already started to transfer the car seats to his vehicle and was bent over while he fixed the first one in place.

"Good morning," she said, letting her gaze rove over his jeans-clad butt. *Very nice.*

"Morning," he said after he'd backed out of the car. He picked up the second car seat and had it fastened and secure in half the time it took her. "In you go, boys," he said. "We have a show to attend."

Yvonne grinned at the mad scramble, although part of her noted her sons' hero-worship in concern. Michael and David had only met Nolan a few times, but he was a natural with them. They needed a man in their lives—not that she intended to settle. Nolan had already let her down once, and she wasn't about to give him a chance to hurt her sons.

Nolan checked the boys were buckled in, then grinned at her and reached for her hand. He tugged her against his chest and started to kiss her before she could voice an objection about her boys' presence. His hands stole up her back to hold her face in place while he ravaged her mouth. Lips, tongue, teeth. His entire arsenal of kissing experience came into play and every one of her objections died a quick death. She looped her arms around his neck and held on for the ride, pleasure setting off detonations throughout her body.

When he lifted his head, his breathing was rapid. She didn't want to think about her reaction. He shifted his hands and tugged off her scrunchie. Her hair released from its tidy ponytail and danced in the soft breeze.

"Much better." Nolan guided her to the passenger door and opened it for her. He gave her a swift tap on the butt of her jeans. "In you go. We have things to do."

"He kissed you, Mummy," Michael said.

"Why did he kiss you?" David asked.

Nolan slid into the driver's seat. "I kissed your mummy because she's my girlfriend."

Damn and blast. "His grownup girlfriend," Yvonne said hurriedly, after visions of phone calls from concerned mothers floated through her mind. Michael was a gregarious soul and made friends easily. Many of them were girls, and she didn't want him scaring them with exuberant kisses. "You can't kiss girls like that until you're eighteen," she added for clarification. She glowered at Nolan when he snorted out amusement.

"Your mother is right," Nolan said as he backed out of the driveway. "You can't do that until you're eighteen." He lowered his voice and slid her a sly look. "Lots of fringe benefits for an eighteen-year-old."

Time for a change of subject. "Gina organized a picnic basket for us. We need to swing by and pick it up."

At the show grounds, Nolan parked his vehicle in the competitors' car park and placed a paper badge on the dash.

"No running off," Yvonne said, turning to face her boys.

"We need to go with Nolan to look at the animals first."

"If you're really good, we'll go on the rides later this afternoon," Nolan said.

The boys jumped up and down, and Yvonne smothered a grin. "You have to behave."

"I'll come back for the picnic basket later," Nolan said.

Spring had arrived much earlier than normal this year, and Yvonne left their coats in the vehicle. She picked up her handbag and fell into step with Nolan. The boys ran ahead, arms outspread like plane wings.

"I enjoyed last night," Nolan said.

Yvonne brushed a lock of hair off her face. "Did you sleep well?"

"I did."

"My work is done," Yvonne said.

Nolan checked on the boys. They were still running ahead, arms outstretched. "What sort of sex toys?"

Yvonne scanned their surroundings before answering. "I have a clit stimulator, a vibrator, a butt plug and some ben-wah balls."

"We haven't tried anal—" Nolan broke off when a group of elderly ladies climbed out of a newly arrived vehicle.

Nolan's mother. *Great. Just great.* If Elizabeth said anything rude to her sons, Yvonne intended to deck the woman. And she wouldn't pull her punches.

"Ah, Nolan," Elizabeth Penrith said. "Good timing. We need help to carry our things to the Exhibition hall."

"It will have to be quick," Nolan said. "I have to help Dad with the cattle we've entered in the show."

"Oh, good," one of Elizabeth's friends said, her stern face softened by gratitude.

"Michael. David." Yvonne summoned the boys to her side.

"Excellent." A third woman with tightly rolled blue curls handed Michael a small blue box. "Can you carry this for me, young man?"

"I don't think—" Yvonne started.

"Nothing breakable," the woman said. "Boys like to feel useful. It keeps them out of mischief."

Yvonne knew her boys and wasn't so sure.

Elizabeth threw visual daggers, and Yvonne ignored them, taking a box of assorted flowers, ribbons and fabric in her arms.

They followed the elderly ladies to a large hall. The cavernous room was abuzz with conversation when they entered, the scent of flowers and baked goods heavy on the air. Some of the displays had obviously been done the previous day. Elizabeth led Nolan, Yvonne and her boys to an area that was currently empty of entries.

"Is this a timed competition?" Yvonne asked the blue-haired lady. Mrs. Williams, she thought, dredging through her memory.

"Yes, and it's always such fun. We have a short time to organize and start at ten."

"Good luck, ladies." Nolan casually snared David's hand and stopped him from racing away down the aisle. His other arm, he slipped around Yvonne's shoulders.

Yvonne almost chortled at the dried prune expression on Elizabeth Penrith's face and cuddled into Nolan, presenting a family unit to anyone who glanced their way. Petty, yes, but she enjoyed it all the same.

Yvonne took charge of Michael, and they wove in and out of men and women carrying flowers, sponge cakes and boxes of jam and chutney.

"My mother has an unerring knack for popping out of the woodwork when sex toys are involved," Nolan said, his voice casual as if he were discussing the weather. "We'll lock the front door and the bedroom door tonight to be on the safe side."

Yvonne croaked, a garbled sound that combined shock with laughter.

"Tyler's here," Nolan said, his pleasure at seeing his younger brother obvious. "And Susan." He swung David up and onto his shoulders and increased his pace to the entrance of the building housing the cattle for show.

Yvonne followed more slowly, slivers of jealousy creeping stealthily into her heart. Susan from the reality show—the woman he'd picked from all the applicants. But he'd chosen her for Tyler, she told herself. The truth didn't help her cope with her envy any better.

When she and Michael reached the group, Nolan was

giving Susan a hug. True, David was involved in the hug, enthusiastically kissing the top of Susan's head too, but still...

Nolan stepped back and slid his free arm around Yvonne's shoulders again, urging her forward. "You remember Yvonne? And these are her boys, David and Michael."

"Of course I remember Yvonne." Susan smiled warmly. Her long, straight hair hung loose around her shoulders and a smattering of freckles showed through her light make-up. Even dressed in casual jeans, a red shirt, black vest and knee-high black boots, the woman glistened with city polish.

"I brought my friend, Christina, down for the weekend. She's here somewhere. You remember Christina, Nolan?" Susan asked. "Ah, here she is. Christina, this is Yvonne, Nolan's girlfriend."

A woman with brown hair, expertly trimmed and highlighted with blonde, shared her grin around. She hugged Nolan, the golden bangles she wore on her left wrist jingling musically. She pulled back and smiled at Yvonne. "I wondered why Nolan picked Susan. Now I know. He was already taken." Christina's eyes twinkled behind the lenses of her glasses.

Yvonne felt her mouth drop open and firmed her jaw. His girlfriend? Nolan hadn't even blinked an eye at the announcement, when in the past he'd hidden her like a naughty secret. And what was with the touchy-feely stuff? Not that she wasn't enjoying his attention, but wasn't their relationship merely a version of friends with very sexy benefits?

"Hey, bro," Nolan said when Tyler joined them. "I hear the farm sold. When are you moving north?"

"In a couple of weeks. I want Katey to start at her school soon. The new owner takes over on the first of next month." Tyler grinned at Susan, his love for the woman shining on his face. "Don't tell Susan and Christina, but Josie and I lured them down here under false pretenses. They're going to help us start packing tomorrow."

Nolan set David on the ground and grasped his hand before he could run amok and upset the cattle in the stalls adjacent to where they stood. "Let me know if you need a hand. Dad and I can both help."

"Thanks! It's mainly the house stuff and tools. The buyer wanted the farm equipment. Have you checked on your entries in the show?" Tyler asked. "I saw Dad. He said one of your yearling bulls had won its class. We've won four of our classes. Eric is ecstatic."

"I'll go and check. Do you want to have lunch together? We can meet on the hill and watch the events in the arena while we eat." Nolan shared his question around.

"Sounds like a plan," Susan said. "Around one?"

Yvonne remained silent while the others made arrangements to meet. Nolan seemed happy spending time with Tyler, when in the past the two had barely spoken to one another. Elizabeth Penrith wasn't a warm person—that was for sure—even though she dedicated her life to raising money for various local charities.

"Let's go and see how we've done with our cattle and sheep," Nolan said. "No shouting, boys. You don't want to start a stampede."

Yvonne smiled when her two boys immediately started firing questions at Nolan, fascinated by the possibilities of cattle in a panic.

By the time lunch arrived, Yvonne had stopped jumping every time Nolan wrapped his arm around her waist. She'd ceased worrying about her boys misbehaving and was equally glad she'd decided on comfortable shoes.

The others were already seated on picnic blankets, the adults with glasses of wine in hand when she, Nolan and the boys arrived.

"Glass of wine, dear?" Josie asked. "And juice for the boys?"

"Thank you," Yvonne said.

Nolan spread out their tartan picnic rug, and Yvonne accepted a glass of wine before busying herself unpacking the contents of their basket. She handed the boys fried chicken legs and a pack of sandwiches before offering Nolan a slice of bacon and egg pie.

"Why don't you come up to Auckland for the weekend?" Susan asked. "Bring Yvonne with you."

"Good idea," Nolan said, his eyes gleaming with sensual promise. "We don't get much time alone."

"I can't foist my boys on Gina," Yvonne protested. "She has enough to do without adding them."

"Make it during the next month, and I'll take them for a weekend," Josie said. "Eric and I enjoy the noise around the place. With Tyler and Katey leaving early, we're going to find it very quiet."

"No, I couldn't—" Yvonne started.

"Don't be silly," Josie said. "You work hard and deserve a break." She turned to Nolan. "You too."

Susan placed her hand on Yvonne's arm and squeezed gently. "Please come. We can have a girls' afternoon. I'm sure Connor—he's one of our friends—will draft Tyler and Nolan to play rugby for his team."

Yvonne hadn't visited Auckland for years. She scarcely got enough time to go to the hairdresser these days, which was why she'd let her hair grow long. "I suppose I could take the opportunity to squeeze in a hair appointment."

"I like your hair." Nolan's gaze settled on the long strands that hung down Yvonne's back.

"Christina is the person you want," Susan said. "She does personal styling and has so many great contacts. Give us a date and we'll arrange it for you."

"Will I get to see the famous *Maxwell's*? Our customers loved that episode of the reality show and talked about it for days. I love to dance," Yvonne said. "I used to do competitive ballroom dancing before I was married."

"You never told me that," Nolan said.

Yvonne winked at him. "Because we're always busy discussing other things." She turned to Josie. "If you're sure about babysitting, I'll take you up on your offer. I'll even volunteer to help with your packing in exchange."

"And I thought this would be stressful," Eric, Josie's husband, said. "Everyone is doing the work for us."

While everyone laughed, Nolan leaned over and brushed a quick kiss on Yvonne's lips. "Thanks for agreeing to a weekend away. It'll be fun."

By the time they trooped around the fairground rides and arrived back at her house, her sons were almost asleep on their feet. Michael bore the remnants of ice cream around his mouth while David had candy floss stuck in his hair.

"Into the bath with you two," Yvonne said briskly while considering the contents of her fridge and pantry. Something quick for dinner.

"Would you like me to handle their baths while you take care of dinner?" Nolan asked.

"You?" She didn't manage to hide her shock very well.

"I know how to have a bath," Nolan said. "I'm sure I can manage two small boys."

"Thanks," she said finally, unsure of how to handle this new Nolan who kept firing surprises.

She showed Nolan where she kept the clean towels and

left him to supervise. From experience, she knew how grumpy her boys became when tired. He'd regret his offer soon enough.

In the kitchen, she went through the motions, frying fish fingers and making mashed potatoes with a side of peas for the boys. For her and Nolan, she cooked pork chops and made gravy. All the while, she listened for shouts and screams. They didn't come. Instead Michael wandered out dressed in his pajamas and settled in front of the television. Nolan and David appeared ten minutes later. David was chattering about the hedgehog he'd seen the previous night and Nolan was smiling.

Yvonne's heart squeezed tight at the way he was soaking up the masculine attention. Damn Jason for leaving her and ignoring the fact he had two sons.

Throughout dinner, Nolan was attentive to the boys and never brushed off their questions. He was equally considerate to her and Yvonne felt a crack open in her heart. She immediately shored up the breach. Nolan had hurt her. Best if she kept things casual.

"Bed time." Yvonne stood, needing time away from Nolan to regroup. She hustled her sons to their bedroom and tucked them into bed. After kissing them goodnight, she unwillingly retraced her steps. She found Nolan in the kitchen. He'd cleared the table and the majority of the dinner dishes were stacked in the dishwasher.

"Alone at last." Nolan prowled toward her, his gaze

twinkling with a sensual gleam of promise. Instinctively, she backed up and found herself trapped between the fridge and Nolan's hard chest. "I've wanted to kiss you all day."

Yvonne thought of the constant touches, the casual kisses that had frequently toppled her off-balance. "You kissed me."

"Not how I wanted," he whispered, his breath warm against her lips.

"But we're just friends."

"We're more than friends."

"No." No, they weren't. A man didn't desert a woman to appear on a reality show, and they certainly didn't do it in the lame way he had. Telling her he had things to do for three months and wouldn't be able to see her. *Huh!* She lifted her chin to glare some of her irritation at the smooth-talking lothario.

Nolan searched her expression. Maybe he didn't like what he saw because he took her mouth in an uncompromising kiss. For frozen seconds, she let him do the work before she began to respond to his expertise. Heck, she wasn't stupid. The man knew how to kiss and she figured she should enjoy the experience—short-lived as it may be. Ditto the toe-tingling sex.

Her hands rose to run through his silky hair as she pressed closer. Such a nice hard body. One only a foolish woman would ignore.

"We can't do this here," he murmured. "The boys."

While she was pretty sure her sons were unlikely to stir, she pulled back and gripped his hand to lead him to her bedroom.

"What about the rest of the dishes?"

"I'll sort them out in the morning." Even though it would throw off her schedule.

"Let's go then." A slow smile bloomed on his lips, fascinating to watch and one that sent waves of fluster crashing through her. Fogged her good intentions.

She couldn't let him take control of this—whatever it was between them. It was necessary to keep the upper hand to save herself from heartache. Yvonne dropped his hand and strode ahead to push open her bedroom door. She flipped on the light and stalked over to draw the curtains. Behind her, he closed the door and the sharp click of the lock engaging seemed like the turn of a key of a cell door.

Deep breath, Yvonne. Take control and throw him off course.

She forced her lips to a smile, pinned it in place and turned to face him. "I'd really like to try out the vibrating butt plug. Are you game?"

He blinked. "We could do that."

"Good," she said. "Why don't you strip off and get on the bed while I get the lube? Would you like to lie on your back or would kneeling on all fours work better for you?"

Nolan made a choking sound. "You want to shove the

plug in me?"

Gotcha.

She restrained her smirk with difficulty and waited a beat while she grappled for control. "I thought we could have turns." *Perfect delivery.* "It's not as if I'm gonna tell anyone. What happens in this bed stays in this bedroom."

His expression had turned impassive seconds after her announcement, and curse it, she couldn't decipher his thoughts.

"You have had anal sex before?"

"Not receiving," he said.

His eyes were burning holes in her, making her wonder if she'd gone too far. "Don't you think you should experience the act from the other side at least once? I have plenty of lube and know exactly what to do. If it hurts you too much, I can stop." Heck, if she laid it on much thicker, she'd start clucking like a chicken.

"You're right," he said suddenly. "I'd love to fuck your ass, but it's only fair if you get to do me too."

Yvonne froze in the middle of mentally marshaling another argument. Had he said she was right?

Nolan started to strip, and bemused, Yvonne picked up the bottle of lube. She squeezed it to within an inch of its life to stop herself reaching for him. Bronzed skin. Long, muscled limbs and that light brown hair with blond streaks. Tight butt, just perfect for forward propulsion. *Be still my heart.*

"You're gorgeous," she blurted. "We always make love in the dark, and I never get to appreciate your sexy body."

The tension noticeably seeped from his shoulders and his grin shone with pure, natural Nolan. "Now that you come to mention it, I don't get to see you often either. Strip, darlin' Yvonne."

Visions of cellulite and a body that had borne two children zapped to the forefront of her mind. Every instinct told her to object, but one glance at his smiling face had her obeying. With the lube set aside, she started to disrobe. Her thick wool socks hit the floor first, followed by her blue jeans and her maroon jumper. Soon she was left in nothing but her bra and panties.

"Keep going," he said, folding his arms over his broad chest.

His brown eyes held a dare she couldn't refuse. Yvonne flicked her bra closure and the cups loosened, gaping forward to display her curves.

"Pretty. Come closer and let me taste those sexy nipples of yours."

Her feet stayed firmly planted. "You're just trying to change the order of events."

"Nope." His good humor sparkled from those big, brown eyes. "You've made a fair point. I wouldn't let just anyone do this to me. I trust you."

Something warm spread through her chest, and she smiled back, prowling over to the bed and halting beside him. His large hands closed on her hips, right above the elastic band of her panties. He craned his neck and captured one nipple between his lips. The draw of his mouth, the tight surge of suction almost took her out at the knees. She grabbed his shoulders for purchase while she savored the swirl of sensations.

"Harder," she said, wanting, needing evidence of his attentions the next day. He released her nipple and sucked a mark on the underside of her breast. Like liquid heat, his touch spiraled down to converge in her pussy. They'd hardly started, yet already her body ached for him and his touch, his presence detonated bursts of pleasure that rippled through her body. Only Nolan. Boyfriends past, her husband...none of them managed to set her afire like Nolan.

He lifted his head, his eyes full of passion and heat. Lust. An answering surge filled Yvonne, and she was tempted to jump him and get to the good stuff. No. She'd go ahead with what she'd suggested, see if her depraved—according to her ex—sexing put him off. Best she learn now.

The truth. She thought he'd enjoy anal sex—she'd make sure he did, and when her orgasm finally came, it would be even more enjoyable due to the wait.

"I love the way you react to my touch," he whispered.

"Are you sure you're up for this?"

His gaze went to his cock, and he smirked. "Be gentle with me."

"Talk dirty to me. Tell me what you're going to do to me, with me."

"You like dirty talk?" he asked in surprise.

"Sounds good in theory. Why don't we try it and see?" Heck, lots of firsts tonight, she thought. "Assume the position."

His baleful look made her giggle, but he knelt on the bed. She noticed his erection had subsided and realized he wasn't as calm as he portrayed. Yvonne picked up the lube and unlocked the drawer where she'd placed her collection of toys. She'd already checked out the instructions and the batteries were fully charged.

When she reached the bed, she saw Nolan's muscles were locked. If she gave a loud shout, he'd probably leap for cover. Although her suggestion was a test, she intended to make him feel good. She slid her hands over his ass and lower to stroke his cock. She kissed the smooth pale skin that didn't see the sun and gradually his muscles relaxed. "This is going to be fun."

"Okay for you," he said drily.

"Don't worry. Once the plug is in place, I'll take you in my mouth and soon you'll feel as if you're flying."

"Promises, promises."

Laughing, she lowered her head and gave into the temptation to nip his ass cheek.

"Hey." His reproving glance made her grin widen.

Yvonne squeezed lube onto her fingers and spread his

cheeks to run her fingers across his puckered entrance, not attempting to enter but intending to awaken his nerve endings, to help him relax. She paid attention to his perineum, pressing firmly. "Talk dirty to me."

"I think about fucking you all the time," he said. "I've never been with anyone like you. You've climbed inside my head. At first, it pissed me off, but I've come to like you there. I love your womanly body and the fact you eat food instead of complaining about diets all the time."

Yvonne listened to his smooth tone and his compliments and the warmth in her chest spread. She dipped a finger inside him, surprising a moan out of him.

"Holy hell," he muttered.

"Don't be a baby," she said, pushing her finger deeper. "You've gone light on the dirty. Tell me how you want to fuck me."

"Hard," he said. "Deep and fast. I want to seize my pleasure, but I want to give in return. I imagine you're just as desperate for me as I am for you. I'm deep inside you, thrusting in full-on strokes. Your pussy is tight, hot, and you're spurring me on, your nails digging into my shoulders."

A quiver went through Yvonne and when she shifted her weight, she smelled her arousal. She slipped another finger into his warm heat and his entire body shuddered. "You okay?"

"Hurts a little."

Yvonne reached to curl her hand around his cock. She pumped his shaft several times while she continued to invade his entrance with her fingers. "You can do this," she whispered, so turned on she was clenching her legs together to try to up the pressure on her clit. It wasn't enough. Her breasts were heavy while her nipples felt tight, needy. Her excellent idea of teasing Nolan had teeth, and they were biting her on the butt.

By the time she'd added three fingers and decided he was relaxed enough to take the plug, she was a mass of writhing nerves. "Keep talking, buster."

He barked out a laugh then groaned when she withdrew her fingers. "That feels weird."

"In a good way?"

"Surprisingly," he said. "When this is finished, I'm going to lick your pussy, gather up all those delicious juices on my tongue."

"Are you going to pay attention to my clit?"

"Just enough to keep you on edge."

"You intend to torture me," she said in disapproval.

"Payback."

After lubing the plug, she slipped it into him. She went slowly, allowing him time to get used to the plaything. With a slow twist, the toy slid into place, the flared base sitting comfortably against his entrance.

"Well done," she said and smoothed her hand over his butt. She moved positions and slipped beneath his kneeling body. His cock was only at half mast, but she intended to fix that and make him come hard enough to see stars. "Are you ready?"

"I thought this was meant to feel good, Kinky Lady."

"It will. I promise." And she sealed her lips around his cock, teasing and licking in the way she knew he enjoyed while she battled the negative connotations his careless name for her held. Past news. *History.*

His breath hissed out, and her urge to grin tugged hard at her restraint, popped her past hurt feelings of her ex. One more surprise in store for Nolan. Without taking her mouth off his cock, she flicked the remote switch on the plug to start it vibrating.

Nolan cursed, and she would have chuckled if her mouth hadn't been full of cock. His shaft grew noticeably and pre-come released on her tongue. She upped her attentions, taking him deeper and moving faster. Yvonne made one change to the remote setting.

"Fuck." Nolan gasped. "That feels...fuck."

His cock grew even bigger and suddenly he was shooting down her throat, his groans and mutters telling her he was enjoying the hell out of this orgasm.

Gradually, she slowed and eased back. She ceased the vibrations of the plug and crawled up the bed so their faces were level.

He didn't comment, instead kissing her with real passion. His weight went down on her as their mouths fused, parted and came together again. When he lifted his head, he teased wisps of hair away from her face and yanked off the scrunchie she'd pulled her hair into while cooking dinner.

"Okay?"

"I liked it," he said. "I didn't expect to."

"You were humoring me."

"I'd do anything for you, Yvonne."

Not true. He hadn't stood for her against his mother—not until recently. He hadn't pulled out of the reality show, and now it was too late. She had to remember that because if he'd done it once, he could do it again.

CHAPTER FOUR

A FORTNIGHT LATER, JUST after midday on a Friday, Yvonne found herself disembarking from an airplane with Nolan and not a kid in sight. When she'd tried to wriggle out of going to Auckland, using the café as an excuse, he'd made a personal appeal to her aunt.

Gina, who never took sides, agreed Yvonne deserved a weekend away from her job and the boys. She'd cut Yvonne's arguments short by saying if Yvonne took a weekend off, then Gina would feel justified taking a break later in the month. Her aunt—the workaholic. Shocked, Yvonne had stuttered her assent, and now she was suffering the consequences.

"Where are we staying?" she asked, once they'd navigated the airport and collected their bags.

"Tyler recommended a place." Nolan wheeled his bag outside and headed for the cab rank. "Susan is expecting our call."

"Have you met her other friends?" Yvonne asked once they were in a cab and on their way to the city center.

"I have. There's Maggie and her husband Connor. Julia is the owner of *Maxwell's*, and she's married to Ryan. You've met Christina already. Don't worry. You'll like them."

"What's *Maxwell's* like?"

"Did you see the clip on *Farmer Seeks a Wife*?"

Hell no. She shook her head, and hopefully didn't reveal the flash of fury that punched through her like a bullet. She hadn't watched the show on principle.

"We filmed a segment there." His gaze bored into her for excruciating long moments, and her heart rate did a little change-up. "You'll see the club for yourself. It's on K' Road and has been in Julia's family for several generations. All the girls—Susan, Christina and Maggie—dance a few nights a week. Julia too."

Yvonne's brows shot upward along with her respect. "Wow." She presumed the costumes were skimpy. "They must be fit."

"Most people hear the word K' Road club and turn up their nose, but it's not like that. The clientele span the ages and you'll see groups of women on their own."

"That's unusual. When I think of a club, a group of horny men comes to mind. Drunk men."

Nolan chuckled and laced their fingers together. Her

heart did another one of those gear changes. Lord, this man was getting to her. She was trying so hard to remain aloof, to keep her scabbed-over heart safe, but he made detachment difficult.

"I thought the worst when Susan announced she was a dancer on the very first day of the reality show. My mind veered in the wrong direction," Nolan said. "You'll see when we visit the club."

Yvonne stared out the cab window at the buildings—first commercial ones, but soon residential properties butted against shops and businesses. Office blocks. "I haven't visited Auckland for years. It's much busier than I recall."

"More traffic too. Is there anything in particular you want to see?"

"Will we have time to catch the ferry to Rangitoto? The boys are keen on volcanoes and Michael wanted to know if we were going to visit."

"Sure, we can do that on Sunday morning. Our flight back is an early evening one, so we have plenty of time. Would you like to bungee off the Sky Tower?"

Yvonne snorted. "You have rocks in your head if you think I'm jumping off a tower, but you go right ahead."

"Just teasing, but I wouldn't mind going to the top. I didn't get a chance to last time I was up here. We should walk to the top of Mt. Eden too. We can get some shots of the crater and some city views for the boys."

The hotel was quiet and luxurious and not far from the harbor. Yvonne gave a gasp when they entered their room. A large king-size bed dominated the space, but the view beyond drew her straight to the window. The blue water sparkled in the sun and yachts raced across the waves, their sails bulging with air. The classical cone shape of the dormant volcano Rangitoto was evident from where she stood, and she knew her boys would have loved seeing the island.

"You'll need to take some photos," Nolan said with a smile.

"I will."

His arm curled around her waist and she managed not to jump. Since the television show had ended, he stroked her at every opportunity. Other people present—no problem. And if they were alone, he still touched her.

Holding her hand.

Tucking a lock of hair behind her ear.

Kisses.

It was those kisses that struck the killer blow. She didn't have any immunity, and damn it, those barricades around her heart kept cracking. The sticking-plaster fixes were useless. They didn't last.

"I'll give Susan a call. Do you want to change first?"

Yvonne glanced down at her jeans. "I didn't bring many clothes. Will I be okay like this?"

Nolan's quick grin flashed—the one that shot a bolt

of lust through her every time she witnessed it. "I was impressed by your light packing. I'm going in jeans, but I know women worry about things like clothes, so I'm giving you the option." He picked up his cell phone and hit speed dial.

Yvonne listened to him speak to Susan. He didn't flirt, but his voice held warmth. She'd heard gossip, of course, even though she hadn't watched the reality show. He mightn't have found love with Susan but their friendship was obvious.

He hung up. "Susan said we can go now and to knock on the door. Do you fancy a walk up Queen Street? We can grab a coffee and something to eat on the way."

"I'd love to walk and window shop. I want to get the boys a small treat. Maybe a toy or a book."

Drawn by the excitement on her face, Nolan reached for her and closed his mouth over hers. His lips lingered as she pressed closer, fitting her curves against his body. He groaned and lifted his head, affected by the simple kiss.

"We'd better go or we'll never leave this room." He hustled her out, and unable to resist, he grasped her hand as they walked through the hotel foyer. He enjoyed the slight widening of her eyes each time he touched her in public, but it also showed him what an ass he'd been before appearing on the reality show.

He'd treated Yvonne like a naughty secret. Even though

he hadn't meant to, he'd demonstrated his lack of care when he'd merely wanted to keep his feelings for Yvonne private. He'd known his mother would assassinate her character because she'd done that with every woman he'd dated. He'd wanted to save Yvonne the drama, the gossip, but in the end his mother had done her worst.

That wouldn't happen again. He wouldn't let his mother's warped mind hurt Yvonne, and damned if he'd let Tyler disappear from his life either. Tyler might live in Auckland, but there was no reason he, Yvonne and the boys couldn't visit.

"What are you smiling about?"

"Just enjoying the moment," he said, sensing if he spoke of what was really on his mind, he'd scare her. She didn't trust him. He got her misgivings, even if his stupidity in letting the wall build between them pissed him off. He needed to work to restore their relationship, to regain her trust.

"There's a bookshop," Yvonne said.

"The boys have lots of books." He steered her past. "Why don't you buy them a T-shirt? Or a model plane?"

"Please," she said. "Have you seen the instructions on those things? Besides, they're too young."

"I'm sure they have models for all ages. What about a football or a game they can play outside now that the weather is warmer?"

"Good idea. I like to tire them out so they sleep well."

Nolan tugged her close and kissed the tip of her nose. "I like them to sleep well too." He'd like it even better if she let him stay the entire night instead of kicking him out after a couple of hours.

Shopping for Yvonne's sons proved more fun than he'd expected, and they ended up buying the boys a puzzle each plus a rugby ball and T-shirts."

Almost two hours later, Nolan knocked on the front door of *Maxwell's*.

Susan opened the door. "You're here," she said. "We're in the middle of dance practice so I won't hug you."

Nolan watched Yvonne's curious face as they followed Susan into the club. It was a big room, but with its midnight blue walls and gold stenciling it looked nothing like a traditional strip club. Tables and chairs waited for the arrival of customers while the bar gleamed. Up on the stage about a dozen dancers went through their paces. Julia stood in front and gave them a wave.

"We won't be much longer," Susan said and ran up on to the stage.

The music started again.

"This reminds me of my ballroom dancing days," Yvonne said.

"Were you good?" Nolan noticed her right foot had started tapping to the beat.

"My partner and I won a few prizes."

"Why don't you jump up on stage and join in? I'm sure

they won't mind."

Her head started to shake in the negative.

The music came to an abrupt halt. "No, like this," Julia said and demonstrated a few quick steps and a leg raise that impressed the hell out of him. "Let's do it again."

"Julia, can Yvonne join in? She used to do ballroom dancing."

"Sure," Julia said.

At the same time Yvonne said, "No, I don't want to get in the way."

"You won't," Julia said.

Yvonne hesitated for a moment before pulling off her vest and unbuttoning her long-sleeved shirt.

An instinctive protest rose in Nolan before he saw Yvonne was perfectly covered by a white tank top. She ran up the side steps and went to the back.

"Dance beside me," Susan said, indicating a space at the front.

Nolan could see the reluctance on Yvonne's face, but she stepped into the gap between Susan and another girl. The music started and after a brief hesitation, Yvonne started moving with the others. Initially, Nolan could see she was a bit rusty, but she soon picked up the moves. Damn, she was good.

"Hey, Nolan."

Nolan turned to see Ryan, Julia's husband, and his friend Caleb. Both men were tall with dark hair and most people mistook them for brothers. Nolan had when he'd first met them. "Great to see you."

"Where's your lady?" Ryan asked.

"Who's the new dancer?" Caleb asked.

Nolan let out a low growl. "Mine. Eyes off."

Caleb grimaced. "Aw, damn. All the pretty ones are taken."

Ryan laughed. "You're too slow, man."

"Women like it slow," Caleb shot back.

"After you catch them," Nolan said. "Slow is no good if you don't catch them first."

Caleb scowled at both of them before speaking to Nolan. "I thought you were a country bumpkin."

"I'm the modern breed. Once we know what we want, we don't mess around."

"So I'm learning," Caleb said. "Your brother snapped up Susan and now you have this lovely lady."

"She's a natural dancer. You're lucky you live in Clare because Julia would want her to work for *Maxwell's*," Ryan said.

She *was* good. Nolan couldn't tear his gaze away and thought she was better than most of the other women.

The song track ended and the women froze in position.

"Much better," Julia said. "Once more from the top, and we'll finish for the day."

The two men left—something about meeting up with friends—and Nolan continued to watch Yvonne. Right now, after watching her move, he wanted to drag her back to their hotel room and get naked. His cock stirred, as if in agreement with his mental musings.

The practice ended and the dancers drifted away, until just Yvonne, Susan and Julia remained.

"You're good," Julia said. "We're one dancer short tonight. I don't suppose you'd agree to go on stage. Two routines. The one we just practiced plus another one. Susan and I can show you the moves. It's a repetitive one—fairly easy."

"No, I don't—"

"She'll do it," Nolan said. "They wear masks. No one will know it's you." The idea of watching her dancing and knowing she belonged to him and other men couldn't have her made him so hot, he wished they were alone so he could show her.

"I'll pay you," Julia said.

"No, I don't—"

"I'll pay for your dinner tonight then," Julia said. "And buy a bottle of Champagne. The good stuff. You have to wait for us to finish at the club anyway. We can't leave until after nine. It doesn't get really busy until later than that, so you wouldn't have to perform for a full house, if that's what you're worried about."

"Yvonne, you did great." Nolan kept his gaze on her face. "Please, I'd really like to see you dance."

"Maggie, Christina and I are dancing tonight," Susan

said. "Julia too. Dance with us. It'll be fun."

"What about costumes?"

"No problem," Julia said. "We have heaps of different sizes."

"I... Are you sure I'm good enough?"

"Yes," Julia said. "I'm the boss, so I should know."

"Good, you're here," Connor said to Nolan from behind them. He set his briefcase on the floor. "We have rugby training in about an hour. Can you come?"

"We'll have to stop by the hotel so I can pick up my training gear." Nolan turned to Yvonne. "Is that okay with you? We could meet back at the hotel, grab a quick snack then come back here."

"We'll drop you back at your hotel," Julia said. "After we sort out your costumes."

Nolan almost smiled when Yvonne hesitated. He tilted up her head to kiss her. It ended too quickly for his liking, when he wanted to drag her to a private place and fuck her stupid.

LATER THAT NIGHT, YVONNE found herself standing on stage beside nine other dancers, her courage dipping, diving, knees knocking while they waited for the curtains to open. The temptation to dance again and embrace a part of her old life had been too much for her to resist.

Her husband hadn't liked her dancing, had said she was making a spectacle of herself and really, she was too big for her partner to lift. Her chin tilted and determination started to pump through her veins. Well, she'd dance tonight. Besides, not even her mother would recognize her in the skimpy red-and-black costume and stage makeup—the pouting red lips, the glittering black mask that screened half her face.

The music started, soft and flirty, and the din of the crowd muted. The curtains swished aside and experience kicked in, the beat flowing through her body. This was a once in a lifetime opportunity, and she intended to squeeze every bit of enjoyment from her Mum-vacation.

Her legs kicked high as she found the seductive rhythm of the music and fell into the pattern of the steps she'd learned earlier that day. Her stage smile slipped into place, and she felt the gazes of the men and women in the audience stroking her body.

She sought Nolan in the crowd and found him smiling, his attention on her, rapt. Her steps faltered before she snapped back into professionalism. Her arms stretched, and she displayed the line of her body. The music segued into faster, sexy.

Yvonne flirted with the crowd, her lips curling into a playful pout. The dancers formed into a line and performed a series of high kicks. Yvonne managed to kick as high as the others and quiet satisfaction flowed through her. She'd feel her muscles tomorrow, pay for the steps into the past. But, oh, it was worth it.

This heady feeling, the buzz of excitement and the taste of success lifting her head high with pride. She bowed with the others, her gaze seeking Nolan again. He was on his feet with the rest of the crowd, clapping with a full-out grin on his face.

"Great job, Yvonne," Susan said once the curtains swished back into place. "I don't suppose you'd consider shifting to Auckland and dancing permanently here at the club?"

"Good try, Suzy," Nolan said, striding onto the stage from the rear and skirting the other dancers as they headed for the dressing room. "Yvonne can dance any time she wants while we're visiting, but I intend to keep her with me in Clare."

A possessive hand landed on her hip, heat burning through her skimpy bathing suit-size costume. Part of her wanted to argue, to tell him he had no right to speak for her, but the truth was she liked living in Clare. The boys were settled, and she owed Gina for extending a hand when she'd been homeless and desperate after her divorce.

"Well," said Susan. "We'll have to entice you to visit often. Bring the boys next time. My cousin is Julia's nanny. She's going to look after Katey as well as Alex. She's really good and won't mind a couple of extra kids now and then." Susan checked on the time. "Julia's doing her fan dance next. Get changed and go out front to watch. It's really something."

"Yvonne." Nolan stopped her with a hand on her shoulder. "You were breathtaking."

Heat stole into her cheeks along with pleasure, his former highhandedness consigned to the back of her mind. "Thanks."

He drew her closer and nuzzled her neck. "And very, very sexy."

"Nolan, stop manhandling my dancers," Julia said in a crisp voice, seconds after she appeared from the direction of the dressing room. Her grin negated her order. "I don't suppose you'd like to move to Auckland?"

"Susan has already tried that," Nolan said.

Yvonne scowled at him and poked her finger into the middle of his chest for emphasis. "Hey, I can speak for myself, mister." She dialed down her frown into a genuine smile for Julia. "Thanks for the offer, but I love living in Clare."

Julia tossed her head and her blonde hair flowed across her shoulders. "Pity. My friends have a knack for finding great dancers."

"I'll see you out front," Nolan said, not chastened in the slightest, judging by his expression. "Would you like a glass of white wine?"

"Thanks." Shaking her head, Yvonne headed for the dressing room and felt Nolan's gaze until she turned the corner.

"Great job, Yvonne," Maggie said. "Here's some makeup remover."

"Thanks." Yvonne removed her mask. "What a rush."

"I know. That's why I dance a few nights a week," Maggie said. "It also keeps me fit. Julia is like a drill sergeant. I've never been in such great shape."

"You should start up dance classes in Clare," Susan said. "The kids really loved the few classes I taught. You could do some fitness stuff for the women too. There's nothing like that in Clare at present."

"The café keeps me busy," Yvonne said.

"Pity," Susan said. "That's a business opportunity going to waste."

Yvonne took a quick shower and changed into her good clothes before heading for Nolan and her glass of wine. Susan walked out with her.

"There you are." Nolan drew her close for a quick kiss.

"At last," a familiar voice said. "My big brother has come to his senses."

Yvonne took a step back and smiled at Tyler. "We're just friends." And maybe if she kept telling herself that, her heart would get the message.

"Good friends," Nolan said in a sharp voice.

Tyler's brows rose, but he didn't say anything.

"How does Katey like the move?" Yvonne asked.

Her question lightened the mood, and soon they were

joined by Nolan's other friends. Julia did her fan dance, and Yvonne watched mesmerized by her smooth moves and manipulation of the large feathery fans. So sexy. Everyone in the club appeared riveted by her dance and when it came to an end, there was a moment of silence before the crowd jumped to their feet and applauded.

"She's good," Yvonne said.

"Susan does the fan dance too," Tyler said with pride.

"Will you teach me?" Yvonne asked.

"Next time you visit," Susan promised.

THE EVENING DRAGGED LIKE a plough resisting rocky soil. Nolan managed to smile through dinner at an Italian restaurant, thought he chatted and acted pretty civilly. But the entire time, visions of Yvonne dancing in her skimpy costume flickered through his head in a never ending video. He glanced at Yvonne—currently chatting with Susan—the feeling of pride bursting to life in him again. It had been a close run thing—the fight between gratification and the urge to leap onstage and drape her curvy body with a long robe.

Now, he pushed the last bite of his veal escallops, Portobello mushrooms and Marsala wine sauce aside and set his knife and fork down at right angles.

"We're going to the restrooms," Susan said.

The two women weaved through the tables of diners and disappeared. Nolan blew out a hard sigh.

"Not hungry?" Tyler asked.

"Have other things on my mind."

"Like what? Farm...oh," Tyler said with an unexpected toothy grin. He shot a quick glance toward the restrooms. "Does Yvonne know you're hung up on her?"

"She thinks I'm playing games until someone better comes along. She keeps telling me we're friends with benefits." He stirred on his chair, repositioning his body to relieve the ache from his hard-on.

Just friends.

"If I hear her say we're friends again, I'll bare my teeth and growl. And that will be just the start. Taking Yvonne out in public is dating, damn it."

Tyler chuckled. "Does your mother know?"

"Yes, not that it's got anything to do with her."

Tyler snorted. "That's never stopped Elizabeth before."

"I intend to marry Yvonne, once she gets over this stupid friend business. Mum will have to accept Yvonne and her boys or she won't have any family left."

"What about Dad?"

"Dad just wants us both to find happiness," Nolan said. "He's changed during the last couple of months. He seems more content and active. Less depressed and moody than we're used to."

Yvonne and Susan returned and took their seats.

"Anyone for dessert? They do an excellent Tiramisu here," Susan said. "The gelato selection is delicious too. Or coffee?"

Good god! He couldn't sit through dessert and coffee. He leaned toward Yvonne. "Do you want to go soon?"

"Already?" she asked in surprise.

In answer, he took her hand and placed it on his lap. She froze, then a saucy grin split her face. "I fancy a coffee. Is anyone else having one?"

A low growl escaped him, and his brother smirked. Nolan shot him a dark scowl.

"Nolan is feeling tired," Yvonne said.

Nolan growled again and decided spanking was looking good.

"He doesn't need to growl like a grumpy bear," Susan chided.

Yvonne cackled. Actually cackled like an evil cartoon character.

"We'll get you a coffee at the hotel," he said, standing abruptly. He didn't care if anyone noticed his *condition*. He handed Tyler a wad of cash to pay for their dinner. "If I'm playing rugby tomorrow I need my rest." He held out his hand in a silent demand.

Yvonne winked at Tyler and Susan and rose. "It appears we're leaving. Thanks for the company."

"Good move," Nolan growled when she grasped his fingers. "If you'd dallied any longer, I would've carted you out dangling over my shoulder, and to hell with the stares."

"Well," said Susan. "I think I'm offended."

"I'm not," Tyler said, and Nolan heard the humor in his brother's voice before they'd left earshot. "We can have an early night now."

The cab ride back to the hotel was mercifully quick.

"That was a bit rude," Yvonne said.

"They're family. Tyler understood." He wrapped an arm around Yvonne and drew her against his side for the short ride to their hotel.

"Good evening. Hey, aren't you that guy on the reality show?" the man behind the desk asked when they walked past to reach the lifts.

"No," Nolan said.

"People tell him that all the time," Yvonne said, laughter shading in her words. "I think the man on the show has a bigger nose. I think he might get a stomach paunch when he gets older."

Nolan grit his teeth and urged her onward. They stepped inside the waiting car. Once the door closed, he moved, crowding her against the mirrored wall. "A big nose and a paunch?" His hands molded her to his body while he claimed her mouth in the way he'd wanted to for hours.

Some of his impatient tension left when her soft lips accepted his, cushioned the hard edge of his kiss. Her eager participation further blunted his frustration. God, she tasted good and the feel of her curves pressing into him...

Damn, this bloody just-friends thing.

They belonged together.

He lifted his head and glared down at her. "You're mine."

Her eyes widened a fraction before they narrowed. "I belong to me."

The lift bell dinged, indicating they'd arrived on their floor. Nolan grasped her hand and towed her to their room. They weren't going to have this conversation in the middle of the hotel corridor.

He wanted to rail at her, the words of dispute lying heavy and rancid on his tongue. Self-preservation and experience told him to save the temper. First things first.

"Has anyone ever spanked you?"

"Huh?" She stared at him.

Was that a hint of intrigue? He liked to think so. "Because, my darling Yvonne. If ever a woman needed spanking, it's you."

He tugged her over to the bed, sat and flipped her over his knee.

"Hey," she said, struggling.

Nolan lifted the hem of her dress to bare her ass. She wore the sexiest pair of panties he'd ever seen. Black lace with a line of white bows down the sides. His palm smoothed over the silky material, and she ceased her squirming.

"Luckily I didn't know what you were wearing underneath your sexy blue dress." He cupped her butt and squeezed. "Does your bra match?"

She sniffed. "That's for me to know and you to find out."

Nolan took a deep breath while he silently acknowledged how much he loved the way she challenged him, her penchant for different when it came to sex. She never bored him. Then he lifted his hand and smacked her perky butt. She let out a satisfying squawk and tried to wriggle from his grasp. He held her firmly and smacked her again at a different angle. The third blow fell slightly lower, and this time she shuddered. Concern struck him for an instant, until he realized she could have put up more of a fight or demanded him to stop. But still...

His finger slipped under her panties to sink into her heat. Wet. Hot. That was all he needed to know. He struck her ass again.

"*Ooh,*" she moaned, the sound so sexy, he spanked her once more just to hear it again.

Her body relaxed, and he smoothed his hand over her bottom, over the silky fabric of her panties and felt the heat of her. He sucked in a deep breath and caught a whiff of flowers with a musky undertone. Her personal scent.

The more time he spent with her, the more he realized she was *it* for him—the woman who made him happy.

"Can you stand?"

"Yes."

He helped her rise and leaned back on his elbows, his legs spread wide. "Strip for me. Show me your sexy lingerie."

Her eyes gleamed, and she tossed her head, her mane of curls shifting with the movement. She bent to unbuckle her sandals.

"No, leave the shoes. I like them."

His compliments didn't hurt either, he noticed.

"Undo my zipper for me. I can't reach it myself." She turned her back to him and his hand shook a fraction before he slid the fastening down.

Yvonne held her dress in place and turned to face him, a bright smile lighting her expression. She let one shoulder of her dress list down her arm, gave him a flirty grin and primly placed it back on her shoulder. She repeated the move with the other arm, giving him a peek-a-boo glance of her bra strap.

"Do you know what happens to teasing women?"

"What?" she asked, her lips quivering as if she were suppressing a laugh.

"They get spanked, and I'm pretty sure the next day they have trouble sitting with comfort."

"Brute," she said, but there was no temper or concern in her tone. "After the dancing, I'll probably need a massage tomorrow. And after tonight, I'll remember the spanking every time I sit down."

"Good." Call him caveman but he rather liked the idea. "I'd be happy to touch you any time. Buy some massage oil tomorrow."

"Bossy much," she said sweetly.

"Strip. Please."

Yvonne released her dress and the fabric slid down her body. A twitch of her hips and it dropped to the floor. She stepped out and stooped to pick up the dress. After setting it over the back of a chair, she turned to face him.

Nolan's mouth went dry and he had to swallow before he could speak. "You're beautiful, and I was proud of you tonight. You looked sexy and powerful and every man in *Maxwell's* wanted you."

She gave her lips a slow lick. "Including you?"

"Especially me." Nolan went to her, his heart thudding against his rib cage. He unbuttoned his shirt and discarded it on the floor. After toeing off his shoes and removing his socks, he stripped off the rest of his clothes. "And now I want to fuck you."

"That's not very romantic."

"According to you, you're not interested in that, but I can do romantic when my balls aren't so painfully tight. When I'm in your pussy and sinking deep into you."

Before she could respond, he scooped her off her feet and placed her on the bed. He followed her down, pinning her in place with his greater bulk. Part of him had prepared for an argument, but what he got was sweet, responsive woman. Her arms curled behind his neck and she met his mouth with hard passion.

He unclipped her bra, eager to get to her curvy breasts.

"Suck me," she murmured.

"Anytime." He shoved the bra aside, deciding to take the time to remove it properly. "I'll take off your panties now too. They're too pretty to rip." Nolan drew them down her legs and dragged in a quick breath. "What—"

"I had to shave because of the line of the costume."

His fingers drifted over the soft skin and slid down her folds into her warm heat. His cock jerked, but he ignored the tightness of his balls. This was something to savor. "I have to taste you." She'd shaved everything and his mouth roved across bare skin, so different from her normal neatly trimmed pubic hair.

"I used to wax when I was dancing but my..." She trailed off and licked her lips before starting to speak again. "The regular appointments are expensive and it's not as if I get time for personal stuff these days."

Nolan made a silent promise to himself. She might be a mother, but that didn't mean she didn't deserve pampering. He could give that to her. He'd enjoy it, although first he'd have to get her past the stupid friends thing. His temper ratcheted up and he had to bite on his tongue to halt harsh words. No. Not when he was so close to getting inside her snug pussy.

He gripped her hips and lifted her to his mouth, his

tongue busily lapping up her sweet honey. His tongue pushed into her and she shuddered.

"More, Nolan. Make me come."

"After you've teased me all night," he said. "I should make you wait." But instead, he slipped two fingers into her, pushing easily into her heat. She was making those sexy little sounds again and lifting her hips up into his touch. He licked her clit, teasing the swollen nub with feathery touches, enjoying the hell out of her taste, savoring Yvonne. They'd been making love on a regular basis, yet right now, he was starved for her, couldn't get enough. He stroked inside her, angling his fingers to hit the right spot, the one that set her off like a firecracker.

"Nolan. Nolan." She gasped and trembled, and he knew it was time to push her harder.

He timed his strokes with the suction of his mouth, the flick of his tongue. Her channel pulsed around his fingers. She cried out and he sucked her clit extra hard. She came apart, the spasms gripping his fingers in tight rhythmic pulses. He lapped at her clit, slow and easy, because he knew from experience she became very sensitive. When the spasms finally ceased, he removed his hand and rose up her body. Her arms came around him in a welcoming hug.

The touch of their lips sent a jolt through him, and her hands squeezing his butt lit him up. All at once, the pressure in his balls was too much. He had to have her now. Nolan levered away from her to grab a condom from the packet he'd placed in the bedside drawer. Fully sheathed, he returned to her and slid between her legs. With his cock positioned, he rammed into her.

One. Two. Three. On the fourth thrust, he started coming so hard he saw stars. A shudder went through him, and the sensations coursing inside him yanked him into savage ecstasy.

Yvonne wriggled and tried to get a hand between their bodies. He stilled her hand. "Please," she said, almost frantically. "Please, I'm so close."

"Let me," he said and levered up so he could see where they joined. He pulled back and pushed into her again because it felt so damn good. He massaged her clit using a gentle touch. She groaned and came almost instantly, her eyes fluttering closed, her cheeks pink from exertion.

"I'm exhausted," she said.

"Go to sleep, babe. It's been a busy day."

She sighed, and her breathing slowed, evened out.

Nolan watched her fall asleep and his heart twisted with a wave of love and possession.

Mine.

CHAPTER FIVE

"Yvonne." A masculine voice floated into her dreams along with the most excellent scent of coffee. "Yvonne." Quietly insistent, the voice grew fingers. They stroked her bare breast, and she came awake with a jolt. Disoriented, her head whipped from side to side as she took in the darkened room.

"Steady, babe."

Yvonne relaxed at the familiar voice. "Nolan. What time is it?"

"Just after nine. Susan and the girls are meeting you at eleven, right?"

Yvonne needed the bathroom. She slid out of bed and almost face-planted when her legs buckled. *"Ow."*

"I thought you might feel sore. I've run the spa bath for you," Nolan said, grasping her arm and holding her upright. "Coffee's ready. I'm starving. Anything you fancy for breakfast? I'll ring room service for whatever you want."

Yvonne tried a step on her own and winced at the spike of pain. "A bath," she said and was a bit embarrassed at the whine in her voice. "Um, coffee."

"I've got that covered," Nolan said. "Go and climb in the bath. I'll bring your coffee in once I've ordered breakfast."

Yvonne limped in the bathroom, took care of business and drank a glass of water. The air was steamy and smelled of citrus. The bath enticed her, and she battled protesting muscles and stiffness to climb over the edge and settle into the water.

"Ohh." She sighed her pleasure as the warmth settled into her sore limbs.

A knock sounded on the door.

"Yes," she said.

Nolan entered with a cup of coffee. Steam curled from the cup, and the scent...oh, the scent.

"Gimme! Thanks," she added when he handed over the cup.

He kissed the top of her head. "Room service will arrive in half an hour." He sauntered out and she twisted her head to watch. The man made her want to bite, to mark her territory—*Stop right there. Friends only, remember? No ownership in either direction.*

With her mind straight and priorities set, she turned her attention back to her coffee.

Yvonne sipped the fragrant beverage, pushed a button to start the jets and relaxed into the bubbly embrace of the water. The sex last night...stupendous. A prickle of sensual tension crawled along her veins as she recalled Nolan's mouth on her, his fingers and cock inside her. She cupped a breast with her free hand and pinched her nipple, before reality tore through her. Jerking upright, she reached for her cup. More coffee. *Now.*

Yikes, something was wrong with her. She was a responsible mother and shouldn't crave sex like this. Like a hungry wild beast, the idea of sex, the doing of it, stalked the recesses of her mind, bringing desperation, longing. She thought about Nolan. She thought about their weekend of freedom from children and drank the last of her coffee before setting her cup aside. Maybe she'd enjoy the ride...

"Nolan?"

"You called, darling Yvonne." The instant he entered the bathroom his gaze went directly her breasts, and she tugged at her nipple.

"I brought my waterproof vibrator with me. I'd like to try it out."

"Only if I get to watch."

Yvonne flashed him a grin. "Done deal. It's in the side pocket of my bag. You can't miss it."

He was back in minutes with the bright blue faux penis. "Looks exactly like the infamous Mr. Blue."

"There was a lot of gossip in the café about Mr. Blue, the vibrator, after that episode of the reality show aired. Mine must be a cousin." She trailed her fingers down her body and under the water to caress her denuded pussy lips. A sigh escaped at the decadent pleasure, and she saw Nolan watching with avid interest. "*Hmm*, that feels *so* good. I need to keep shaving or start waxing again."

"Yes."

Her grin widened, and she held out her hand for her vibrator.

"Why do I feel as if I'm superfluous to requirements?"

Something in his tone irked her, lifted her chin in defiance. "You're not always going to be around. What happens when you decide you've had enough of fun and sex with me? I've got two children, responsibilities. You're a single male."

Nolan let out a string of curses, his large frame tensing in the doorway while he squeezed her vibrator in his right hand. "Hell, you have no idea what I think."

Yvonne sat up in the bath and glared at him. "One of us has to be sensible, look to the future."

"I thought I'd made it clear," Nolan said, irritation burning off him in palpable waves. He looked down at his hand and flung the vibrator at her. "I want you and the boys in my life. This isn't a temporary thing for me."

Some of the starch went out of her and she sank beneath the warm water again, her nakedness suddenly making her feel vulnerable. She gripped the vibrator tightly in her hand. "You threw us away quickly enough last time, and that's why we can never be more than friends. The boys and I aren't disposable. When I decide I need a man in my life full time, I have to be sure he'll stick. I've already made one mistake, and I don't intend to muck up again."

"So none of this—us—matters to you." Temper turned his mouth into a cruel slit, and she wished she could magically conjure up a barrier of thick clothes. This wasn't the perfect place to pick a fight.

"Of course it matters. We're friends." Unease crept into her seconds after the words left her mouth. That wasn't quite true. Her stupid, traitorous heart kept trying to turn their camaraderie into more. *No.* No sentimental crap for her. She bore no illusions about her pull on the opposite sex. Heck, her husband had left her for another man. What did that say about her sexual allure?

A thump at the door indicated the arrival of room service, and Nolan stomped away with another curse. Yvonne set the vibrator aside and grabbed a white flannel. She added soap and briskly washed herself. Five minutes later, she pulled a cotton robe around her and padded out to join Nolan.

"More coffee?" he asked, his tone abrupt, his mouth precision straight.

"Thanks." *Talk about uncomfortable.*

"Scrambled eggs? Toast?"

"Yes, please." Yvonne flinched at the politeness. *Great. Just great.* "What are you doing this morning?"

"I'm meeting Tyler and helping him shift furniture around at his new place."

Yvonne nodded. "That's nice." Awkward silence fell. "I'm sorry. I—"

"Don't." Nolan made a slashing motion with his hand. "Not when you don't mean the apology."

"You walked away from me." Yvonne felt the sting of tears in her eyes and fiercely willed them away. She would not cry.

"I didn't walk away. I explained I couldn't see you because of the reality show."

"The premise of the show was farmers seeking a wife!" Her voice emerged in an unattractive screech, and she snatched a breath, fighting for equilibrium. She let the air ease out to the count of three before locking gazes with Nolan. "Believe me, I got the message." When Nolan didn't answer straightaway, she poured herself another cup of coffee and stood. "I'll go and get ready. I don't want to keep the girls waiting."

His mouth firmed and he gave a clipped nod.

She felt a wave of petty satisfaction at being the one to leave, then the emptiness, the wrongness struck her. Damn, she hated arguing. She hesitated, sighed, and continued to the bedroom. Trying to discuss this further right now would only spoil both their days.

NOLAN WALKED THROUGH THE Remuera house at his brother's side. He was meant to be admiring the native timber and the size of the place, but his thoughts centered on Yvonne. "Yvonne and I had a fight." He dragged a hand through his hair, frustration churning his stomach. "Damn. I didn't mean to blurt that out."

"Oh?" Tyler said, the rise of his brows indicating curiosity, a willingness to listen.

Nolan hesitated and studied the man who was his half-brother. Tyler wouldn't gossip, and he needed a man's opinion. "She keeps saying we're friends and according to her, that's all we'll ever have."

Tyler leaned against the doorjamb. "What do you want?"

Nolan shuffled uncomfortably and stalked into the oblong-shaped room, his boots thudding against the wooden floorboards. "I want her, the boys in my life. They make me happy."

"Have you told her you love her?"

"I—" Nolan came to an abrupt halt and spun to stare at his brother. "Fuck."

A grin spread across Tyler's face. "You don't get bent out of shape like this if you don't care. I figure you must love her if you're thinking of a future, but you need to tell her.

She's not a mind reader."

Nolan heaved a sigh, the idea feeling newer than it should. But it wasn't as if he or Tyler had received a good demonstration of the finer emotions between adults. He couldn't recall his parents embracing. No, their interactions were generally sniping matches.

"I've hurt her. Before the reality show, we were seeing a lot of each other. I used to spend quite a few nights at her place." He scowled. "Somehow Mum got wind of it and she started spreading rumors about Yvonne. Then Mum entered me in that stupid show and I decided on payback. I should've explained things better. Instead, I backed off because I wanted Yvonne out of Mum's firing range."

"Bro," Tyler said, his tone sympathetic. "A woman mightn't understand. She wouldn't see you were trying to protect her."

"You think? How the hell am I going to fix this?"

"You're asking me for advice?"

"Quit being a smartarse and help me."

"Tell her about Dad and Elizabeth, about me. Explain you were coerced into doing the show and wanted to protect her."

"And if that doesn't work?"

"Play the long game and show her by deed. Be her friend, and when the right opportunity presents, tell her you love her."

"And if she doesn't believe me?"

Tyler clapped him over the back. "The long game, bro. If you really love her, then she's worth fighting for, worth taking a few knockbacks. As long as she isn't seeing anyone else, you're in with a chance."

Nolan nodded, seeing the sense of patience even though it galled him.

Later that afternoon, he and Tyler drove to the rugby grounds and prepared for the game. When they ran onto the field and he scanned the sidelines, searching for Yvonne.

"Enough of that," Connor said, nudging Nolan sharply in the ribs. "Mind on the game. Sexy women come later."

YVONNE ENJOYED THE RUGBY game. She stood on the sideline with Susan, Christina and Maggie clapping and cheering each successful drive and run the Hawks made toward the try line.

"What's the score?" Julia asked, breathless and beautiful with Ryan and Caleb in tow.

"They're actually winning," Maggie said without taking her gaze off the game. "Connor will be so excited. Go, go!" she screeched when the Hawks got the ball. It flew from player to player and everyone cheered until one of the opposition did a head-high tackle on Tyler.

"Boo!" Susan shouted, and the supporters on their side

of the field echoed her cry.

"Penalty," Maggie said, seconds later. "I wonder if they'll kick for a goal or decide to run the ball."

Yvonne joined in the banter, her earlier sullen mood gone after shopping with the girls and her hair appointment earlier in the day. They were in Auckland until the following evening, so she might as well make the best of things. No matter what Nolan said, she couldn't risk getting hurt again. Marriage—well, she'd thought she was getting forever when she said "I do" and look at the result. Her husband and her dance partner.

The final whistle blew, and the Hawks' supporters jumped up and down in excitement, applauding wildly.

"We've won a game," Maggie said. "Twenty-one to three. It's unheard of. We need to celebrate."

"Later at the club," Julia said.

"Is anyone going to the clubrooms with me?" Maggie asked.

"I will," Christina said.

"I'm going back to the hotel room to have another hot bath. My muscles are killing me," Yvonne said. "You girls have tired me out."

Susan gave her a quick hug. "I'm going to head off too. Want to share a cab with me? Maggie, can you tell Tyler and Nolan we've gone?"

Back at the hotel, Yvonne ran the bath and gathered her hair into a topknot, pinning it in place so she didn't get it wet. Her morning visit to the hairdresser might have been expensive, but her dollars were well spent. The man had wanted to cut more off the length, and she was still wondering why she'd listened to Nolan's plea to keep her hair long.

The bubble of the spa bath eased the ache in her arms and legs, and once dressed in a new pair of black trousers and a tunic top, she felt heaps better. She made a cup of peppermint tea and sat by the window in the late afternoon sun. The harbor was a busy place with ferries sailing over to Devonport and off to places farther afield. A tall ship drifted in the distance, the sails billowing with wind.

The door opened. "Yvonne?"

"I'm here," she said, setting her tea aside and standing.

Nolan came to an abrupt stop. "You look beautiful."

Pleasure sizzled at his compliment. She'd thought she looked good, but Nolan was devouring her with his gaze and her confidence soared.

He stepped closer. "Can I kiss you?"

Relief threatened her knees. She gave him a bright smile, happy that their argument seemed consigned to the past. His hands drifted over her hair, now highlighted with golden streaks and about four inches shorter. The hairdresser had also layered it to give shape and take out some of the weight. He smiled and leaned closer to rub their noses together before taking her mouth in a slow and thorough kiss.

"We need to talk," he said eventually. "But I don't want to spoil the rest of our weekend by arguing. No," he said when she started to speak. "Let me just say this, then we'll get back to the enjoying part. I want to be more than friends with you. I understand I've hurt you, and I need to make up for that. Let me prove to you how good we are together."

"I don't understand." His kiss—so full of sensual promise—had addled her brain, making it difficult for her to concentrate.

"I know, sweetheart. I want to be your husband, and I'm willing to wait until you're sure of me."

"But—"

He placed his hand over her mouth to halt her confused words. "I need a shower. I decided to head back here after the game. Do you fancy a walk along the waterfront? We could have a drink at one of The Viaduct bars."

"That sounds nice," Yvonne said.

"Great. I won't be long."

Yvonne stared at his back as he sauntered away, her brow knit in bewilderment. He wanted to marry her? She'd thought...

Heck. Friends, yes. Sexual benefits, yes. But marriage?

She'd gone into her first marriage with blinkers firmly intact. Sure, she'd experienced happiness during those years and she had her sons, but the way her marriage had ended still played with her confidence. She found herself stalking to the bathroom.

"You want to marry me?" she demanded, bursting into the steamy warmth.

"Yes," he said over the sound of the water.

Yvonne sank down onto the edge of the bath, the chill of the porcelain beneath her bottom and the brief flash of discomfort in her butt cheeks driving her to her feet again.

"Not right now, but in the future. Once you've realized I'm serious about you, about us and the boys. And maybe we could add a little girl to our family."

"Oh." She found herself biting her bottom lip and stopped. He hadn't mentioned love. She opened her mouth to ask and reconsidered. No. She agreed with him about one thing. She wanted to enjoy the rest of the weekend, and if he said he didn't believe in love or some other such male thing, she might hit him. That *would* spoil the weekend.

He turned off the water and opened the door to snag a towel. "You really do look beautiful. I like your hair very much."

Yvonne hugged the sincerity of his compliment to her heart. "It's been a long time since anyone told me that."

"Really? I've slipped up then. Because not only are you beautiful, but you're sexy as hell. I've half a mind to drag you to bed and show you exactly how I feel about you."

The pleasure in her deepened and took on an edge

of sexual excitement. "You're pretty sexy yourself, Mr. Penrith."

"So I'm on a promise for later tonight?" His wide grin threatened her knee stability and she reached out to hold onto the door.

"Count on it," she said and sashayed back to her cup of peppermint tea.

CHAPTER SIX

BACK IN CLARE, YVONNE slipped into her daily routine. Days passed and Nolan didn't mention marriage again, although he spent a lot of time at her house. Sometimes he stayed late. Sometimes he left as soon as the boys went to bed. And sometimes, like today, he took half an hour and stopped by the café for coffee and one of Gina's savory muffins.

"Everyone's staring," Yvonne said under her breath.

"Let them." Nolan shrugged without concern and placed his hand on top of hers.

Immediately Yvonne heard the rise of whispers, sensed the exchange of I-told-you-so glances.

"They'll get over it soon enough. Would you like to go to the pub for lunch on Sunday? It'll be me and Dad, plus Eric and Josie since it's their last day here in Clare."

"What about the boys?"

"It's a family lunch," Nolan said, squeezing her hand. She saw his lips twitch at the flurry of muted words that floated from the elderly ladies sitting at the next table. "Of course the boys are invited."

"I'd like that," Yvonne said.

"Good. I'd better go. Some stupid idiot took the corner too fast and went through my fence. I patched it last night, but I need to pick up a coil of wire and batons and do a proper fix."

Yvonne stood and started to gather their empty cups.

Nolan touched her arm and smiled. "I'll see you later tonight. Probably after the boys go to bed." Then he kissed her, a quick, brief kiss that did little to quench her desire for physical contact, yet made her tingle all over anyway. "Be good."

Yvonne laughed. "That gives me plenty of leeway." She watched him until he disappeared outside before clearing their table. The acute silence pierced her happiness bubble, and she glanced up to find herself the focus of the café customers. Most wore smiles and approval. "Show's over, folks," she said and gave an elegant bow. Applause followed her out the back.

"What's going on?" Gina asked, looking up from rolling out pastry. A dusting of flour covered one cheek and a few wisps of iron-gray hair curled from beneath her chef's hat.

"Nolan kissed me goodbye in front of everyone."

"Good on the boy. I wonder how long it takes that to get

back to Elizabeth."

"I don't want to talk about that woman," Yvonne muttered. "And she'd better keep her broomstick away from me."

Gina gave her pastry another pass with the rolling pin, then turned the oblong with deft hands. "That woman is judgmental. Always has been and I doubt she'll change, although you'd think she'd learn after driving both sons and her husband away. I heard Samuel is going out with Daphne Chester."

"Really? That must be difficult for Elizabeth. They're not divorced yet."

"He's visited the lawyer," Gina said. "Daphne told me that. She wouldn't go out with him otherwise."

Yvonne let out an indelicate snort. "This town is a hotbed of gossip. What with the feud between the O'Grady's and the Drummonds, the Penriths' split and the Shakespeare sextuplets coming home to do a reality show, the local tattletales are spoiled for choice."

"You forgot to add the Mathesons," Gina said, her tone dry. "The original Matheson was a real black sheep, and they say the daughter takes after her ancestor with all her shenanigans."

"I don't think I've met her."

"No, she's been overseas for a while. You'll know the minute she hits town." Gina cut rounds of pastry and lined tins. "Can you grab the meat pie mix out of the fridge?"

Yvonne retrieved the covered dish of steak and onions in thick gravy and handed it over. "I'd better get back out front before the natives get restless."

"Is it serious between you and Nolan?"

Yvonne stopped halfway to the door and turned to her aunt. "He says he wants to marry me."

"I don't see a ring on your finger."

"I told him I wanted friendship and that was all."

"Yet you let him kiss you in the middle of the café where people can see. The locals have already started a sweepstake. I thought I might take a punt, but you need to give me the inside scoop." Her aunt let out a sharp cackle. "You should see your face."

A call went up from the front. "Yvonne!"

"I'm needed," Yvonne said in a dignified voice. She left to the sound of her aunt's hoots of amusement.

Yvonne kept busy with making coffee while her assistant took orders and cleared tables. In the bookstore section, customers browsed the shelves and the cash register pinged its happy song every time the assistant rang up an order. Business was booming since the reality show. Clare seemed to have hit the tourist map big time.

The doorbell announced a new arrival, and Yvonne glanced up. She fumbled the jug of hot milk she was heating and burned her hand. "Damn."

Yvonne turned to grab a can of cold soft drink and held it to her smarting skin while she spied on Elizabeth Penrith.

The woman waved at her circle of friends—the same ones who'd whispered and witnessed the earlier kiss—before stalking to the counter to place her order. Why the devil had they started coming to *Gina's Books*, anyway?

Yvonne surveyed the pinked skin and decided she'd live. She went back to building her order of coffees. Low murmurs floated to her, but she firmly ignored her impulse to lift her head and glare. If she shrugged off gossip, people would soon tire of her and move on to the next juicy tidbit. As Gina said, they were spoiled for choice.

"Good morning, Yvonne," a cool voice said.

Yvonne's hand slipped again and hot milk sloshed on the back of her hand. "Bloody hell," she muttered, letting the cup go. It wobbled, and in slow motion, toppled to the floor. *Damn and blast.*

"I'm so sorry. I didn't mean to startle you," Elizabeth said.

"Good morning, Mrs. Penrith," Yvonne said, and hoped her bared teeth bore a resemblance to a polite smile.

"Please call me Elizabeth. I'll let you get on. I can see you're busy." The woman's grim countenance lightened and the corners of her mouth lifted. She gave a nod and trotted away to join her friends.

Yvonne stared, and aware of the renewed whispers, started picking up the larger pieces of broken china.

Gina appeared seconds later, gave the floor a swift look and made a clucking sound. "I'll get a mop," she said, and retreated to the kitchen.

Later that night, Nolan rushed through the door, bringing with him the cool of a rainy night. Yvonne raised her head for his kiss, recoiled at the touch of icy lips.

"You should have stayed at home. It's miserable outside."

She took his coat, shook off the worst of the rain before hanging it up on the empty hook next to her boys' jackets. Should she tell him about his mother's weird behavior?

"This is home for me, Yvonne." His gaze was steady on hers as he said the words, his sincerity blazing through. "When I think of home, you and the boys are the first things that come to mind."

"Oh, Nolan." His words undid her, tore away the makeshift patches on her heart. With two quick strides, she reached him and flung her arms around his neck. Like a monkey, she clung to his large body, uncaring now of the chill.

"Let's go to bed," he whispered against her lips.

"It's early."

"Who said anything about sleeping? We'll warm up."

A gurgle burst from Yvonne. Tinged with happiness, it surprised her, shocked her since she couldn't recall the last time she'd made that saucy sound of compliance. Nolan swept her into his arms and headed for her bedroom. He shut the door with his hip and deposited her on the bed. He followed her down, caging her in his arms, taking possession of her mouth. Hunger exploded between them—hot and molten, urgent.

She flicked her tongue against his, the move provocative and earning her a sensual growl.

"Wait. I'd better lock the door. Do you want me to check on the boys first?" He punctuated his words with a slow hip swivel. The throbbing hardness of him scored her belly, and instinctively, she wriggled until they notched together in perfect alignment.

"I'll go." Yet she didn't move, couldn't move when her heart ached with fullness.

He lifted away, his grin one of masculine satisfaction. "I'd like to see the boys. They look angelic when they're asleep and recharging."

"Nolan," she whispered so softly she knew he wouldn't hear. She rolled over to her side, hugging herself in an effort to contain her joy. In little ways, he'd edged into her life—some might compare it to an insidious disease. His methods contained that sort of silent creep. Despite her or in spite of her, he'd grown roots here and wrapped them around her heart, around her sons until they'd all started to accept him, to miss him when work kept him absent.

She'd cleared a hook for him on the coat rack.

Nolan had transformed this house—her and her sons—into a home. The final barrier around her heart let go with an inaudible whoosh. It allowed a sliver of fear through to nip at her happiness. She wanted to tell Nolan she loved him, but he hadn't said the words either, and she couldn't help remembering her husband, contrasting the two.

Her husband had professed his love. He'd told her they'd have a happy life, forever.

He'd lied.

"The boys are sound asleep. Hey, those look like heavy thoughts." Nolan tugged a lock of her hair.

She blinked up at him. "Sorry. Busy day at work. Sometimes it's hard to switch off." And that was a big, fat lie. She was stupidly letting her past mess with the possibility of a happy future. Nolan loved her. He loved the boys, and he demonstrated the depth of his feelings every day, in every interaction. Michael and David were thriving under his attention, and she shouldn't need his words to rubberstamp the deal when words were like cheap carnival beads. Actions were the gold in this treasure hunt.

"Let's get you into bed then," he said, his kindness bringing the sting of tears to her eyes. Not the impression she wanted to give tonight. Crying would raise questions, and she needed to shore her defenses.

Another thought whisked into her mind, one she hadn't entertained for a long time, and an unwelcome blast from her husband past.

You're kinky, Yvonne. Admit it. You like trying new things, pushing sexual boundaries. The only time you didn't

disgust me was when you agreed to a threesome with your
dance partner. That time you played right into my hands.

"Yvonne." Nolan shook her lightly. "What's wrong?"

"Nothing," she replied automatically, and it was obvious to both of them she'd told a fib. She pushed out a grumpy sigh, angry at her ex all over again and pissed at herself for letting *him* spoil her time with Nolan. "The past."

"What about it?"

"Forget it," she said. "Nothing important. I'd rather show you how much I missed you today." She reached for his buttons and unfastened two. Time to deflect his curiosity. She leaped into siren mode, which was what she did best, and dipped her fingers beneath the denim of his shirt. Warm skin. She leaned closer to kiss that skin and masculine soap and the faint whiff of farm wrapped around her senses like her comfortable flannel robe. "I want you."

"I'm yours." He sucked her bottom lip, gave her a quick nip. A low moan sounded deep in her chest. It rushed up her throat, shoving aside every misgiving, every hesitant thought. She tugged his shirt and struggled to remove the garment.

Nolan laughed, not even trying to help her search for more skin and farm-fit muscles. Instead, he trailed tiny kisses down her throat, lingered at the juncture of her shoulder and neck until arrows of heat and pleasure darted through her to sink into the bull's eye. God, she wanted him. *Right now.*

Busy hands dealt with her clothes while his mouth paid homage to every erogenous zone he revealed. The swish of his tongue tickled her stomach. A puff of warm air down her folds sparked a tightening sensation deep in her womb, and she stirred restlessly, splaying her legs and displaying everything to his gaze.

For a second, thoughts of her husband threatened, her muscles tensing when she recalled his disgust of sexual intimacy with her, his dislike of her open enjoyment.

Yvonne cursed under her breath, angry with herself for letting her husband intrude yet again. Almost defiantly, she lifted her hips in a silent demand for more of Nolan's touch, and his hum of approval shunted her to a better place. One hand fastened on her hip and held her still while he finally made contact. She sighed in pleasure at the languid, lazy swish of tongue on and around her clit.

"More," she demanded and barely jumped when the fingers of his other hand roamed to press against her puckered entrance.

"How much more?"

"Everything, Nolan." As his thumb pressed deeper, an edge of dirty heat knifed her, stealing her breath, stopping her heart for an anxious moment. Need warred with decorum. "I haven't done this for a long time."

Nolan lifted his head, his eyes glittering with lust. "Do you want me to stop?"

Yvonne forced a smile, kicked husband memories in their fleshy gut. "Just go slow."

"I would have anyway," Nolan said with a quick grin of acceptance. "You went easy on me. Lube?"

"In the drawer," she said, indicating which one with a jerk of her head. He gave her nub a lick and continued down, teasing her pussy, his stubble rasping the delicate skin of her inner thighs. The spicy tang of arousal filled the air while he drove her higher with his fingers and mouth.

When he finally rose to grab lube, the hot pleasure from his touch made itself felt in sensual pins and needles. Her nipples were hard, distended. Ruby red, and the touch of her hand at her breast arced down to her pussy in a bungee of raw, needy demand.

"Yvonne, that's so hot. I love watching you, your open sensuality. I like your sense of adventure. It makes loving you fun."

Eyes she hadn't remembered closing flew open, opposing adversaries of guilt and pleasure battling it out for supremacy. She gazed at Nolan, tried to register his mood, his thoughts, the reasons and meaning behind his words.

And failed.

Her judgment had warped, leaving her like a boat bobbing on an ocean and not an oar in sight. She could no longer trust her gut.

Nolan frowned.

The silence lengthened until it snapped like a dry piece of pasta.

"My husband thought I was kinky, and not in a good way." *Oh, god. Now she'd done it.*

Nolan stared, searching her features for explanations.

She had nothing more to give.

"You don't talk about him. I figured you'd relegated him to the past, which is fine by me. His stupidity gives me the chance to scoop up you and the boys for myself."

"I like sex." *Shut up now, Yvonne.*

"So do I," Nolan said with an easy shrug. "What's not to like? I enjoy the way you take the lead sometimes." He picked up her hand and pressed a kiss to her knuckles. "I love the things we do together. Sex with you is exciting and fresh." Nolan stroked her hip as he spoke, his touch soothing the doubt beast but not slaying the monster. When she bit her lip, he leaned over and kissed her, taking her mouth hard. His tongue swept inside and danced against hers, demanding a response.

Swept up by his passion, Yvonne surrendered, her arms creeping around his neck. She rocked against him, trapping the hard length of his cock between their lower bodies.

He groaned against her mouth, and she couldn't help her spurt of amusement. Nolan jerked away, his stern expression belied by the twinkle in his sex-on-his-mind eyes. "I'm directing matters today." He pinched one nipple as if to ascertain her attention. "On your hands and knees. You have my permission to play with your clit while I'm preparing you."

"Yes, sir." *Good plan.*

"I like that," he said, and when she turned over to follow his instruction, he smacked her buttock.

"Hey."

"That's for letting your mind go to your ex while we're getting busy." The sharp crack of his palm hitting her bottom rang out. "Don't do it again. We'll talk afterward. Understand?"

"Yes, sir." Yvonne found herself grinning, despite the tingle of heat at her butt.

His hand came down again, hard enough to smart. "Make sure you remember it."

Nolan shifted his weight. The *whurt-whurt* told her Nolan was pumping lube from the bottle. Seconds later, his finger pressed against her entrance.

"Ooh." She attempted to wriggle from his grasp. "You could've warmed the lube."

"Now where's the fun in that?"

Yvonne sucked in a breath, let it ease out slowly and forced relaxation on her rebellious muscles. Her butt throbbed, her pussy ached and the bore of Nolan's finger tunneling into her ass completed the trifecta. She inhaled, let the air whisper back out.

"Okay?"

"Better than I remember."

"That's because it's me," he said, full of smugness.

"Big head."

"Yes," he said. "And soon it's gonna be inside you."

A snicker burst from her, counteracting the sensation of pressure and the dance toward pain.

"I thought I told you to play with yourself."

Her clit was engorged, slippery and every nerve ending vibrated. Sweet anticipation. Nolan had more than one finger in her now, the aching bite falling on the good side of the pain barrier.

"Give me a running commentary. Tell me how you feel."

"Good. I can feel the stretch from your fingers. There's a bit of pain. Not too bad. When I touch my clit the discomfort backs off."

"I'm going to get more lube."

Once again, the chill against her skin made her flinch. Nolan laughed softly and gave her another finger, working her easily. She delved between her legs and alternatively tugged on her nipples. The ache...the need for more grew to desperation levels.

"Nolan."

"It's okay, sweetheart."

"I need you inside me."

"It's time." The rip of a condom package, his easy agreement tripped her pulse rate. The grumpy protest of the lube bottle made her catch her breath.

"Ready?"

"Take me. Please, take me."

He fit his cock to her, and she relaxed, trying to keep her breaths even. Slow. The hard length of his cock pushed inside her, her guardian muscle protesting. Fire swarmed over her, intense bursts of heat. He pulled back, tunneled deeper. The faint sensation of pain twisted through her, a lash of erotic fear before she calmed and remembered to stroke her clit.

Finally, finally, his warm weight draped over her back, and he started to fuck her in earnest. Each stroke pushed her to the slim border between pleasure and pain.

"You're so beautiful, sweetheart. I love the feel of you squeezing my cock. Such a dirty girl. My sexy, dirty girl," he whispered against her ear. "You feel good. So good. Not gonna last much longer. Stroke yourself again. Make yourself come. I want to feel your arse clenching 'round my dick. Want to come so bad, sweetheart."

Mesmerized by his voice, she sank into a pleasure zone as she fingered herself. The clawing tension in her pussy increased, the delicate brush of her fingers and the fullness in her arse, pushing her hard. Bright sparks of sensation came slowly at first, a burst of awareness.

Nolan pulled back and stroked smoothly into her. He gave a hushed moan and it ricocheted through her straining body, pushed her harder, faster and the swell took her, hauling her into a maelstrom of pleasure that left her sobbing.

"Nolan." Her finger kept working her clit while her vagina and arse pulsed hard.

Nolan gave a hoarse groan. He pulled back, sank deep. "Can feel the spasms around my dick. Feels good." His hips snapped forward in three rapid thrusts and she gasped, her rectum clamping around him hard as he froze. Her clit jumped in another mini climax and a shudder rocked her.

Only the hoarseness of their breathing broke the silence, and for long moments, Nolan rested against her back. He sucked her neck, and she knew it would leave a mark.

She didn't care what others thought.

Nolan pulled from her, turned her to face him. "I love you, Yvonne. You're everything to me, and if you think I'm letting you get away, think again. I want to marry you."

She seized on the first part of his declaration. "You love me?"

"You doubt me?" Nolan sat back, frowned at her. "Back in a sec."

Yvonne fell forward to sprawl in a boneless heap. Some parts of her body ached while others felt well-used. *Nolan loved her.* She tested his words for sincerity and ended up hopelessly confused.

Nolan returned, and she heard the snip of the lock. He switched on one of the bedside lamps. "Let me get you cleaned up."

The warm cloth was blissful, and a sigh emerged as she let him tend her. Task completed, he tossed the cloth aside and climbed into bed. His arms wrapped around her, and he arranged her against his chest. He tipped her chin upward and their gazes connected. "I haven't said this before, because the words hold power. They mean something to me. I love you, Yvonne, and I want to share my life with you and the boys. Wait." He placed his fingers over her lips. "I haven't handled things well between us. I've made mistakes, but I've learned from them. I can't imagine my life without you in it."

He stared at her in silent expectation.

"I love you too, Nolan." There, she'd voiced the feelings that struggled for freedom. "But I need to take things slowly. I don't want to rush and have the boys hurt."

"I would never hurt your sons." A wounded expression settled on his features.

"I know that." She gave a heavy sigh. "I'm not explaining myself well. You say you want to marry me. Would you consider an engagement?"

His eyes narrowed. "How long?"

"Just give me three months."

"What's gonna change in three months?" Now he sounded belligerent.

"My husband told me he loved me. He said he intended to spend the rest of his life proving it to me."

"Don't try forcing me into your ex's shoes."

"I'm not." Yvonne paused, reordered her mind. "My husband was always telling me my enjoyment of sex wasn't right, that I needed help. I know there's nothing wrong with me. I have a healthy sex drive, and I'm not about to apologize for the fact."

"It makes me a lucky man."

Yvonne hesitated, her mind darting to previous mistakes. A question trembled at the tip of her tongue, one she'd thought about, considered and reconsidered since the breakup of her marriage.

If you don't ask you'll never know.

But she hated the sudden insecurity that made her ask, the way she was tarring Nolan with wounds from her past and testing his commitment to her and the boys. The damage inflicted by her husband had settled deeper than she'd realized, but she had to be sure she didn't repeat history.

She wanted a man who wanted and needed her.

Just her and no one else.

She cleared her throat and let the words spill out. "What if I asked if we could have a threesome with another man?"

"A ménage a trois?"

"Yeah." An Irish dancer was doing a jig in her stomach.

"No." He stared at her, his eyes hot, suddenly untrusting. "*No.* I won't share you with another man."

She stared back, her gaze locked with his. This sounded like a man who didn't intend to reconsider. *Ever.* "What if

I suggested another woman?"

"No."

"You haven't even thought about it."

"And I don't intend to either. Other men might be okay with sharing their wives or girlfriends, but not me. I want a woman of my own." His expression might have been a smirk on another man. Yvonne knew better. Not an ounce of emotion traveled to his eyes. "I'm not good at sharing. Ask Tyler. The only exception would be sharing my life with you. That would be easy."

"So no women either?"

Nolan grasped her shoulders and shook. "No. You want extra penetration or different sensations, we'll invest in more toys."

"My husband suggested a threesome," Yvonne said. "I thought it'd be fun. Our marriage had been on shaky ground for months, and I figured it was worth a shot. I thought it might bring us closer together."

"What happened?"

"It turned out my husband had the hots for my dance partner. And it became obvious my dance partner returned the sentiment. I became an unnecessary third in the bed. I—I don't want that to happen again."

Nolan bolted upright in the bed, his eyes flashing with temper and shock. "This was a bloody test?"

CHAPTER SEVEN

ANGER TOOK A CHOKEHOLD on his throat, thrummed through his veins. She didn't believe he loved her, and she'd set him a fuckin' test. But it was her lack of trust—like a knife to his heart—that slashed his outrage most.

"What would have happened if I'd agreed to a threesome?" he snarled. "How far would you have let it go?"

The guilt in her face said it all. "I wouldn't—"

"Ah, just enough rope to hang myself." Nolan saw his boxer-briefs and pulled them on. His jeans were in a crumpled pile by the bed, and he grabbed those too. He jerked the denim up his legs and snatched his shirt off the floor. The entire time he was dressing Yvonne didn't say a word. "I couldn't win, no matter what I did."

When she still remained silent, he let himself out of her room and left. He stomped to his vehicle and peeled out of the driveway, his foot pressed on the accelerator.

Damn the woman.

Nolan found himself heading toward town and ten minutes later, he screeched into the pub car park. One drink. He'd have one drink. He strode into the pub and stalked up to the bar.

An hour later, the barman cried, "Last orders."

Nolan looked at his glass and realized he hadn't drunk more than two mouthfuls of his beer. The amber liquid had lost its white head and appeared flat and unappetizing. He pushed it away and headed for his vehicle.

In his truck, he pressed his forehead against the steering wheel for an instant and squeezed his eyes shut.

Damn the woman.

Why couldn't she have trusted him?

YVONNE STARED AT HER bedroom door and winced. She'd handled that badly, known she was making a mistake, but like a train wreck, she couldn't seem to stop herself from asking the question about threesomes, from pushing until she received the necessary reassurance to obliterate every one of her doubt demons.

God, she could still recall the humiliation when she'd climbed out of her marriage bed and her husband and best friend hadn't even noticed her departure. In the kitchen, back then, she'd poured herself a glass of wine and sat down trying to work out where her marriage had gone so wrong.

It was obvious her husband had felt nothing for her any longer, and she'd wondered if he'd ever loved her. In hindsight, she realized her husband's mother had seemed more excited about the marriage than her son.

Sighing, Yvonne pulled on her robe and padded out to the kitchen. Wine had done the trick last time. Maybe it would help this time too.

"Mummy. Mum!"

Mother's instinct had Yvonne jerking awake with a start. The abrupt movement sent jagged shards of pain on a frantic journey through her head. She moaned as other parts of her body transmitted pain—her neck, her shoulders. Her stomach. *Eek!* A blast of bright light seared her eyeballs when she forced her lids to open.

"Are you sick, Mummy?" Michael pushed his face close to hers and backed away just as abruptly. "You don't smell good."

David hovered behind his brother, his expression bearing concern. Yvonne forced a smile even as she attempted to tamp down the nausea doing an energetic dance in the pit of her stomach. "What's the time?"

Michael squinted at the clock on the far kitchen wall and chewed his bottom lip. "The big hand is pointing up." His brow furrowed. "Ten o'clock," he said triumphantly.

Yvonne's head snapped around to check for herself. Ten to eight. Her shoulders slumped with relief. Late but doable. "Let's get you ready for school and kindergarten."

"We dressed ourselves," David said.

"And you did a great job. We'll comb our hair after breakfast." After downing two glasses of cold water, Yvonne organized breakfast cereal for the boys and quickly assembled their packed lunches.

She grabbed a quick shower and then she and the boys were out the door, only a little behind schedule.

Half an hour later Yvonne entered the café.

Gina was seated at the counter, a cup of coffee at her elbow while she read the paper. She took one look at Yvonne and grunted. "Rough night?"

"You could say that."

Gina stood and walked around the counter to pour another cup of coffee. She added milk before handing it over to Yvonne. "Are you sick or have you had a fight with Nolan?"

"Nolan," Yvonne said tersely. "Do we have headache tablets somewhere? I couldn't find any at home."

"I have some in my handbag," Gina said. "Stay there. I'll get them." She disappeared and returned a few minutes later to hand over the tablets. "What did the boy do this time?"

Yvonne swallowed two and washed them down with coffee. "He didn't do anything."

"Then—" Gina's eyes narrowed on Yvonne. "You did something."

"I don't want to talk about it."

"Fine, but drinking doesn't solve anything."

Temper flared in Yvonne. "I know that." She scowled into her coffee. "I had a momentary memory lapse."

Gina gave a bark of laughter and it echoed painfully inside Yvonne's head. "My muffins aren't getting made while I'm sitting here. Make sure you eat something. You'll feel better."

"I sincerely doubt that." Yvonne barely suppressed her shudder at the idea of food.

The headache tablets and sheer determination got her through the day, and she picked up the boys from the after school sitter and headed home with the intention of an early night.

"When's Nolan coming?" Michael asked.

"He's gonna make a kite," David said.

"He's probably busy with farm work," Yvonne said. "Why don't you build a castle out of your blocks instead?"

Crisis averted, Yvonne started baking a chocolate slice to go in the boys' lunch boxes. She kept herself busy and slipped into bed just before nine. At an uncivilized hour of the morning, she woke and her mind bolted straight to Nolan. No matter how hard she tried to shove the memories away, the wretched man refused to leave her thoughts. His smile. His touch. The gentle way he interacted with her children.

The sexy times...

A quiver of awareness shot to her pussy, the sharpness of her need bringing a moan.

Damn, the man. For the long months after the death of her marriage, she'd made do with her vibrator. Up until she'd met Nolan and decided to let him into her bed, she'd purchased batteries every week during the grocery shop. Now Nolan wasn't here and she knew from experience—their break during the reality show—that fresh batteries in her vibrator didn't do the trick anymore.

Nolan was the magical ingredient.

He made her happy.

He made her boys happy.

Damn.

Shoving aside the insistent yearning, she turned over, rearranging her body. A few seconds later, she twisted again, restless and unable to sleep.

At six, she gave up the fight and climbed out of bed. By the time she woke her sons, their lunches were ready and breakfast was on the table.

"Will we see Nolan tonight?" Michael asked.

"I think he's very busy at the moment," she said.

"We'll visit him," her younger son said.

Yvonne's heart did an agitated blip while her throat closed in dread. "Eat your breakfast," she managed. "It's a school day."

"We could go on the weekend."

"Maybe," Yvonne said while cursing inwardly. Her sons were like pit bulls when they attached their minds to something.

When Yvonne walked into the café after dropping off the boys, Gina was in her normal spot, reading the paper and enjoying a quiet coffee before the regulars started arriving.

"Have you sorted things out with that man of yours yet?" Gina's sharp gaze sliced and diced, her mouth pursing as she figured out the truth for herself. "I should knock your heads together."

"Just leave it alone. Nolan and I...it's not meant to be. He doesn't want me."

"Did he tell you that?"

Yvonne blinked rapidly. No way did she intend to cry and compound her problems. "He left. That's all the answer I need." Yvonne turned away and tried to shut up a conscience that had suddenly turned yappy. Like a small persistent dog, her mind went back and forward and her moral code kept wavering to Nolan's side.

She'd been the one in the wrong.

What she'd done was unforgivable because Nolan was nothing like her ex. Time and time again, he'd demonstrated his sincerity. Her boys loved him, and she…

Damn and blast.

Yvonne blinked hard, misery determined to pull tears from her blinking eyes.

"Ring him," Gina said. "Apologize. Do whatever it takes to get him back."

Yvonne stiffened and turned to glare at Gina. "Why should I apologize?"

"You're not going around muttering it's his fault, ergo you're the one who stepped out of line. Besides, you admitted it yesterday when you were dragging your heels with a hangover. Apologize."

"Ergo? Who the heck says ergo?"

"Apologize." Gina stood and folded her newspaper. "I'm off to make bacon and egg pies."

Yvonne stared at the front door of the café. Someone was waiting outside, checking their watch. Sighing, Yvonne grabbed her apron and tied the strings as she walked to the door.

"What have you done to Nolan?" Elizabeth Penrith subjected her to a hard stare before she brushed past and took a seat at the counter. "I'll have a…a latte with non-fat milk."

"Good morning to you too." Yvonne stomped behind the counter and started bashing her coffee machine around. It was only the start of her day.

"Nolan is going around in a blue funk. He's depressed.

He told me to butt out of his life and leave him alone."

"And you're not listening to him," Yvonne snapped.

"He's my son. You want the best for your sons, and it's no different for me."

Yvonne started heating the milk. "There's a difference between caring and wanting the best. You tried to break us up. You spread rumors about me and called me a loose woman. You judged me when you know nothing about me." By the end, she was shouting. The internal door squeaked as Gina popped out from the kitchen.

"Is everything all right?" She wore flour on her cheek and several smudges of an unidentified substance on her apron.

"I'm standing up for myself," Yvonne said.

"I'm sorry," Elizabeth said. "I haven't been fair to you. Nolan has been different since he met you. He's happy, or he was until recently. I don't know what has gone wrong between the two of you, but if it's something to do with me, please make up. I want family. I want grandchildren to spoil." Tears swam in the older woman's eyes as she stared pleadingly at Yvonne. "I don't want to be alone anymore. I've had to take a good hard look at myself recently, and I didn't like what I saw."

"You what?" Yvonne was pretty sure she resembled a fish, and she forced her lips together while she stared at the woman. "You've tried to break up Nolan and me for ages, and now you want us back together?"

Elizabeth chewed the last of the pale peach color off her bottom lip. "I understand my about face has shocked you, and I'll need to earn your forgiveness. I intend to try. That is a promise."

"I see." Had she tumbled into Alice's wonderland?

"Please, talk to Nolan," Elizabeth said, and there was a quiet dignity to her manner.

Gina, her children and now Elizabeth Penrith—all of them thought she and Nolan should be together.

"I'll take your views under consideration," Yvonne said.

"Don't be so stubborn," Gina said.

Elizabeth sent her a hopeful glance. "No time like the present."

"I can't go now. I need to man the counter."

"I can do it for you," Elizabeth said. "I don't know how to make coffee, but I can take orders and clear tables."

"I'm almost done with the cooking. If Elizabeth doesn't mind pitching in with kitchen chores as well, we'll manage between us."

"But—"

"Go." Gina pointed at the door. "Leave the apron here."

Yvonne dug in her heels when Gina tried to shunt her toward the door. "I don't know where to find Nolan."

"He's working at the cattle yards with his father. They're drenching a herd of cattle. If you go straight there you'll make it before they start on the next chore."

Yvonne scowled at both women before focusing her

irritation on Elizabeth Penrith. "Apologizing doesn't negate everything you've said and done in the past. I'm going to reserve my decision when it comes to you."

Elizabeth nodded. "That's all I ask. It's more than I deserve."

Yvonne stared at her for a bit longer, confused—no, shocked—by the woman's change of heart, despite her explanation. That saying about leopards and spots not changing...people were the same. They didn't transform character flaws overnight. She tugged her apron over her head and handed it to Gina.

Gina tugged her close for an uncharacteristic hug. "You love Nolan. Even an old unromantic like me can see it. Don't let stubbornness get in the way. The pair of you are good together."

"I..." If she hadn't messed things up too badly. Nolan might decide to wash his hands of her, and she wouldn't blame him if he did.

She found herself at the cattle yards almost too quickly, certainly before she'd decided exactly what to say. She parked her car and climbed out, a burst of nerves punching through her and pebbling her skin with goose bumps. Nolan was working the race, sending stock into the chute and making the task look simple while his father wielded the drenching gun. Mr. Penrith inserted the barrel of the gun at the corner of the animal's mouth and released the worm medication before moving on to the next beast. The pair worked like an efficient machine.

"Nolan, visitor," his father called above the bawl of a cow.

Nolan's gaze traveled to her, and he straightened momentarily. "Be with you as soon as we finish."

Yvonne nodded. She should've grabbed a few coffees and something for the men to eat before she left. She watched Nolan, noted his capable manner as he worked with the cattle. Although she'd known he was a farmer, she'd never visited him during a day of farm chores. He teamed well with his father, and soon the cattle had all gone through the race and stood in the larger, outer pen.

"Dad, I'll move the cattle if you want to go into town. Could you pick up some more drench while you're there?"

"Sure thing. See you later, Yvonne."

"Are you in a hurry?" Nolan asked in a cool tone. "I don't want to leave the cattle in the pen without water. It will take me half an hour to shift them."

"Can I help?" It was better than standing there like a ninny.

"See the gate down the road? The brown one on the right?"

Yvonne squinted into the sun. "Yes."

"That's where I'm taking the cattle. Drive down to open the gate, then stand in the middle of the road and turn the herd into the paddock." He walked away before she could reply.

Okay. She eyed the cattle dubiously before bursting into action. No longer a city girl, she figured she could do this. Wait until she told Michael and David. They'd be wide-eyed and impressed. And they'd want to help the next time. The boys were already thriving in Clare, and they missed Nolan. Every night so far this week they'd asked when he'd arrive, their disappointment clear when she'd fobbed them off.

Yvonne drove past the gate, parked her car and jogged back to the gate. When the cattle neared, pushed forward by Nolan's calls and his dogs, she stood in the middle of the road and hoped like hell they didn't decide to run her down. They looked bigger on this side of the fence.

"I don't think I'd make a good farmer's wife," she blurted once the gate was safely shut. On wobbly knees, she closed the distance between them. Last week she would've hugged him. Today touching didn't seem appropriate. Between last Saturday and today, she'd lost the privilege.

"Oh," he said, his dark brows rising in polite inquiry.

She stared at him and got it. He wasn't going to make this easy for her. "Nolan, I'm sorry for letting my crappy past destroy what we had together. The boys miss you. Gina has been lecturing me all week and today your mother came into the café to add her five cents to the subject."

"I see." Nolan whistled his dogs and walked away.

"Nolan." His name was a verbal protest.

His shoulders tensed and he halted, but he didn't turn to face her.

"Is that it? I screwed up. I get it. Hell, I screwed up royally, but people make mistakes. I forgave you when you made me look stupid in front of the entire town, yet I don't get the same pass?"

Nolan turned around them, emotions flickering over his face so fast she couldn't read him. His fists knotted at his sides, and she got the impression he wanted to punch something. Someone. "You said you were sorry, but not once in your little speech did you say anything about being here because *you* wanted to. It was the boys, Gina, my mother."

"Oh for goodness sake." She did an eye roll. "Can't you read between the lines? I love you. I've missed you like crazy, and the second you walked out on me I wanted to run after you."

"Why didn't you?"

"Because I'm an idiot," she snapped. "Because my pride told me you'd come back." She moved half a step closer, willing him to meet her halfway. He didn't move a muscle. "Are you accepting my apology?"

"Yes."

"And?" No mistaking her tone for anything except testy.

His expression relaxed suddenly into a smile, but he remained unmoving. "Are you going to suggest having a threesome again?"

"No! I don't want to share my man with anyone."

"Am I your man?"

"Yes, damn it! How many ways do you want me to tell you I'm sorry? I love you. I know I've hurt you, and I'll try really hard not to make the same mistake again."

"Will you marry me?"

"Is that a proposal?" He didn't answer and she stared at him in frustration. Damn, the man. She leaped at him, and she silently cheered when his arms wrapped around her to hold her steady. "Yes, I'd love to be your wife."

"That would make you a farmer's wife."

Yvonne wrinkled her nose. "I guess I could learn if I had the right teacher. Maybe your father could—"

"I'd be quite happy to spank you," Nolan said in a confidential manner.

"*Ooh*, kinky."

"With you." Nolan brushed his fingertips over her cheek, the delicate touch bringing a wash of tenderness and love. "Only with you."

And then he kissed her, and everything in her world righted. His arms around her felt true. Perfect. His lips against hers fueled lust, love and made her think of forever.

He lifted his head, his crooked grin and the warmth in his eyes bringing relief and happiness.

"Thanks," she whispered.

He pressed his forehead against hers. "You'll make a

great farmer's wife. Can I come around tonight?"

"Come for dinner. Stay the night if you want."

"The boys?"

"They'll need to get used to having you around." She tugged at a lock of his hair. He needed a haircut. A wife could remind him. "Somehow I don't think they'll mind."

NOLAN ARRIVED BEFORE IT was time to pick up the boys.

"You're early," Yvonne said.

He prowled toward her, a man confident of his welcome, and she laughed in delight when he scooped her up and carried her to her bedroom. She grinned up at him when he dropped her on the mattress.

"Are we doing kinky today?"

Nolan stripped off his shirt and went to work on his footwear and jeans. "Not today. We'll save that for another time."

His cock was fully engorged and ready for action. Yvonne's hands went to the hem of the uniform polo shirt she wore for work.

"No, let me." He kissed her hard, the pressure of his lips and the sleek thrust of his tongue signaling his intent. Moisture pooled between her legs as she surrendered to him. She was his.

The second he'd dispensed with her clothes, he brushed

his fingers over the fullness of her breast. She held him to her as he bathed her nipple with his tongue then sucked hard. With every touch, desire climbed inside her and they hadn't even reached the good stuff yet. Nolan trailed his fingers lower, parted her legs and slid one thigh between hers. She quivered with the rush of cool air on her damp folds. Making love with Nolan always sent her flying, but this time seemed extra special.

"You're so beautiful," he whispered.

"I love you."

His expression softened. "I know. You didn't think I was going to let you get away did you?"

"What?" She gaped, saw the upward tilt of his lips and the humor sparking to life in his eyes.

"I love you too much. I intended to give you time before I stormed the fortress again."

"You make me sound like a battleship."

"No." He bit her nipple, the sensations exquisite. "Mine."

Chills chased across her flesh, the achy need between her thighs growing bigger, more. "Don't use a condom," she said, seeking his gaze and connecting with his wide eyes.

"But don't you want to wait?"

"I've waited for you for a long time already." Yvonne pressed a kiss to his pectoral muscle and sank in her teeth hard enough to make him start. "What do you say about a baby girl?"

"Are you sure?"

Yvonne cupped his face and drew him down for a kiss. "I've never been surer of anything in my life."

He groaned, deepening their kiss. Desire, liquid and molten bounced between them. He nuzzled her throat and guided his cock to her entrance. His fingers branded her flesh as he pushed inside. "Yvonne, you feel perfect—hot and tight around my dick." He pushed deeper, the friction between their bodies almost unbearable. Never had she scaled the heights of passion so quickly, and she trembled with urgent need.

Yvonne gripped his rump, felt the flex of his muscles when he embedded himself fully. The curl of arousal spiraled low in her belly, expanding when he withdrew and drove deep again. Hot, sensual flames licked up her middle, and he gave a rough growl as he upped his pace. He pushed her body deeper into the mattress, and she clung to him, trembling with the ecstasy of his possession.

"How close are you?"

"Really close," she said.

"Touch yourself. Let me feel your finger against the base of my cock."

Yvonne slipped her hand between their straining bodies, rubbed, and when he drove into her body again the coil of energy rippling through her snapped. Bolts of pleasure streaked to her toes, and she gasped. "Love you, Nolan."

His cock pulsed against the walls of her vagina and his

shaft seemed to thicken. He groaned and stroked into her again hard and fast. Once. Twice. His face contorted in a mask of pleasure, his big body quivering with the punch of his climax.

"Yvonne." He stole her next breath with his kiss, the uneven thumping of his heart keeping time with her own pulse rate. "God, Yvonne. That was amazing."

She grinned at him. "Think how much better it will feel with practice."

"Cheeky minx." He pulled out of her and tugged her against his sweaty body. "I was serious about spanking you."

Laughter bubbled through her as she winked at him. "As long as the spanking comes with cooling lotion and cuddles afterward."

They lay quietly together, his arm brushing up and down her spine.

"I need to move soon and pick up the boys."

"What say we both go to collect them? We have time to drive to Napier and buy a ring. The boys could help us choose, and we could celebrate with dinner before we head back to Clare."

Warmth flooded her, and she found herself smiling and tearing up at the same time. "That's a great idea. Michael and David would love the treat, and they'll be so excited that we're all going to live together."

His eyes were bright with happiness. "Are you okay with

moving to the farm?"

"Of course."

Nolan gathered her in his arms and the atmosphere thickened between them. She pressed a kiss to his neck and reveled in his possessive hold, the stroke of his hand and the renewed surge of his cock against her stomach.

"We don't have time for a quickie," she whispered, a hint of laughter in her voice.

"No problem. We have the rest of our lives."

"The farmer has found his wife," she murmured.

"Damn straight," Nolan said. "And this time I'm keeping her."

PLEASE TURN THE PAGE for a glimpse of *Enemy Lovers*, the next book in my *Friendship Chronicles* series.

EXCERPT — ENEMY LOVERS

WHOA. DALLAS O'GRADY CAUGHT a glimpse of blonde hair seconds before the woman kicked her flat tire. She owned the sexiest arse he'd seen in months. Without another thought, he pulled his truck onto the shoulder and climbed out to offer assistance.

"Problem?"

"My brother is an idiot." Her lyrical voice held the same crisp chill of the wind whistling across the Napier road. She turned, and he caught a friendly smile belying her words. "Thanks for stop— You!"

The smile skidded away.

Hard drops of rain fell on Dallas's face, the sleeves of his brown leather jacket, as he eyeballed a very sexy, very grown-up Laura Drummond. His gaze shifted to the gray, washed out clouds, the sky building to dense black on the horizon, then to the rear tire on her late model sedan.

"Fine, if you don't want my help, I'll be leaving."

"No, please." Her hand shot out to halt his retreat. "I'm sorry."

"Sorry you're hobnobbing with the enemy?" He spelled out what they were both thinking. Their parents would issue horrendous battle cries if they witnessed this scene, saw the pair inhaling the same air, let alone engaging in something civil like a conversation.

She swept a strand of blonde hair away from her pink lips. "You're not my enemy. I don't know you." She stuffed her hands in her jacket pockets, hunched her shoulders against the rain and stamped her feet. "Look, I'm grouchy. I have a flat. My brother borrowed my spare last week and told me he put it back. My phone is dead, and I'm not going to make Clare in time for my cousin's hen party. My mother will make dolls in my image and stick pins in them."

"My brother said there's a landslide partially blocking the road leading into the town, near the Shannon Pass. If it keeps raining, they might close the roads, if they haven't already. You wouldn't make it even if your car was drivable."

"Yep, I'm screwed," she said.

No, she wasn't—not yet, but he'd love to take that thought to its logical conclusion. While their families might harbor long-standing grudges, his dick wasn't sticking with the program. The skinny Laura Drummond from his vague school-day memories had grown into a classy woman. Her brown eyes glinted with intelligence while her mouth...

Dallas tore his gaze off her because his inappropriate thoughts bore repercussions. For one—a painful hard-on. And two, no way could he cozy up with the enemy.

He cleared his throat. "What do you want to do? I can give you a lift to Clare and hope we'll make it past, or I can ring for a breakdown truck."

The rain was coming down harder now, icy crystal pellets pummeling his cheeks. She caught her bottom lip between her teeth, worried it then nodded a decisive agreement.

"Let me grab my purse and overnight bag," she said. "I'll grab a ride and chance my luck. The landslide might have been cleared already."

Dallas told himself not to look, but when she bent over to retrieve her bag, his eyes zeroed in on her arse.

Down boy.

God, he hadn't experienced this sort of reaction to a woman for a long time. He wanted to fuck her. He wanted to fuck her mouth, holding her in place by her hair, and most of all he wanted to tie her to his bed. He wanted the classy Laura Drummond to submit to him while he fucked them both to breath-stealing pleasure.

Shaking the lust away, he accepted her bag and stowed it behind the driver's seat. He straightened, his mind leaping straight to her and sexual desire. Man, he was weak. Giving in to his libido, he watched her lock her sedan and splash through puddles to join him.

"You don't resemble your sisters and brother." They were dark-haired, her sisters both shorter than Laura.

"Nope, everyone says I'm the cuckoo in the nest." She peeled off her wet raincoat and slid her long legs into his vehicle. "Ugh, it's bucketing down out there. I'm lucky you came along."

She was still talking when Dallas climbed behind the wheel. Nervous? He grunted, started his truck and pulled on to the road, trying to ignore the unpleasant sensation of water dripping down his neck.

"I take after my great-grandmother on my mother's side. They say I'm her twin."

Dallas nodded while his mind trotted back to the more pleasant occupation of imagining this woman naked and engaged with him in things carnal. A whoosh of heat replaced the chill of wet clothes.

"What are you going to do if the road is closed?" she asked.

"My cabin is on this side."

"Oh."

"Are you wondering what I'm going to do with you if the road is closed?"

"Please." A strangled laugh emerged from her, tinged with a healthy dose of uncertainty. "I doubt you'd do away with me."

"But you're not too sure?" He set the window wipers to a faster speed and eased up on the accelerator, not taking his attention off the road. "I am one of *those* O'Gradys."

"Positive." She slanted him an ice-princess look, lifted that elegant nose just so. "I'm pretty sure you're not hiding horns under your hair, although you might be concealing a tail. Even so, I'm confident I'll get through this ordeal unscathed. I'll grab a ride back to Napier. There's bound to be someone heading to the city."

Dallas barked out a laugh, amused at her sly humor lurking beneath the hauteur. She didn't act like any Drummond he'd come into contact with in the past. He'd thought he might have consigned himself to an hour of chilly silence—more than an hour in these driving conditions. But she'd tossed his assumptions on their butt, and he found himself wanting to explore her mentally. Ditto the physical.

"What do you do for a job?" He shot her a quick glance, caught the wrinkling of her nose.

"My mother organized a place for me at a charity. I'm working for them at present, but I'd prefer a position with more challenge."

"What sort of employment are you looking for?" Hearsay said Laura's older sisters had never worked in their lives. They'd done the socialite thing, found rich husbands and married. They were now popping out a new generation of Drummonds to heap down hate on the O'Grady family.

"I enjoy organizing things, which makes me a natural in the administration field."

"Are you good with computers?"

"Not bad. Any program I don't know, I can learn. I'm a quick study." Her chin lifted a fraction as if she expected him to challenge her statement.

Again, he found a smile pushing his lips for escape. He enjoyed a woman who surprised him. "If you weren't a Drummond, I'd offer you a job."

"What sort? What do you do?"

Again, not the reaction he'd expected. "My brothers and I own a couple of Irish bars in Napier, and I have several rental properties. It's getting too much for me to handle the paperwork along with the day-to-day things." The pub where he had his office wasn't in the best part of town. Nah, he couldn't see Laura slumming it at *O'Grady's*. "We're thinking of buying the old pub in Clare."

"The one that closed down due to fire damage?"

"Yeah." Dallas peered through the windshield, not taking his eyes off the road.

"Can I interview for the job?"

Dallas slowed even further until his truck crawled. Closer to the Shannon Pass, the rain slapped the windows, obliterated the scenery. What he could see of the sky was a sullen gray and lightning flashed in the distance, followed by a rumble of thunder. "You want to work in a pub? Maybe I should check *you* for horns and a tail. You have an impish sense of humor."

"I'm not joking," she said, and he felt the weight of her gaze. "But if you want to check me for devilish signs you go right ahead. I might enjoy it."

Dallas opened his mouth, shut it again, risked a swift glance in her direction. A tiny grin played around her luscious lips. Oh yeah. She was pleased with herself. "I'm an O'Grady, sweetheart. I don't possess the right bloodlines for you."

Do Dallas and Laura tempt fate?

Read Enemy Lovers to find out.

(www.shelleymunro.com/books/enemy-lovers/)

ABOUT AUTHOR

USA Today bestselling author Shelley Munro lives in Auckland, the City of Sails, with her husband and a cheeky Jack Russell/mystery breed dog.

Typical New Zealanders, Shelley and her husband left home for their big OE soon after they married (translation of New Zealand speak - big overseas experience). A twelve-month-long adventure lengthened to six years of roaming the world. Enduring memories include being almost sat on by a mountain gorilla in Rwanda, lazing on white sandy beaches in India, whale watching in Alaska, searching for leprechauns in Ireland, and dealing with ghosts in an English pub.

While travel is still a big attraction, these days Shelley

is most likely found in front of her computer following another love - that of writing stories of contemporary and paranormal romance and adventure. Other interests include watching rugby (strictly for research purposes), cycling, playing croquet and the ukelele, and curling up with an enjoyable book.

Visit Shelley at her Website
www.shelleymunro.com

Join Shelley's Newsletter
www.shelleymunro.com/newsletter

OTHER BOOKS BY SHELLEY

Fancy Free

Protection

Romp

Buzz

Festive

Friendship Chronicles

Secret Lovers

Reunited Lovers

Clandestine Lovers

Part-Time Lovers

Enemy Lovers

Maverick Lovers

Sports Lovers

Military Men

Innocent Next Door

Soldiers with Benefits

Safeguarding Sorrel

Stranded with Ella

Josh's Fake Fiancée

Operation Flower Petal

Protecting the Bride

Bundle

Military Men

Alien Encounter series

Janaya

Hinekiri

Alexandre

Bundle

Alien Encounter